NINE LADIES DANCING

Twelve Days of Christmas

Emily E K Murdoch

ARE YOU SIGNED UP FOR DRAGONBLADE'S BLOG?

You'll get the latest news and information on exclusive giveaways, exclusive excerpts, coming releases, sales, free books, cover reveals and more.

Check out our complete list of authors, too!

No spam, no junk. That's a promise!

Sign Up Here

www.dragonbladepublishing.com

Dearest Reader;

Thank you for your support of a small press. At Dragonblade Publishing, we strive to bring you the highest quality Historical Romance from some of the best authors in the business. Without your support, there is no 'us', so we sincerely hope you adore these stories and find some new favorite authors along the way.

Happy Reading!

CEO, Dragonblade Publishing

Always the Widow (Book 9)
Always the Rebel (Book 10)
Always the Mistress (Book 11)
Always the Second Choice (Book 12)
Always the Mistletoe (Novella)
Always the Reverend (Novella)

The Lyon's Den Connected World
Always the Lyon Tamer

Pirates of Britannia Series
Always the High Seas

De Wolfe Pack: The Series
Whirlwind with a Wolfe

CHAPTER ONE

"D ON'T PUSH ME!"
"Careful with that bag, it has my favorite gown—"
"Oh, the decorations look marvelous!"
"Well, Chalcroft always looks its best at Christmas…"

Nestled at the top of the wide, sweeping staircase that over-looked the great hall, Olivia smiled down at the gaggle of people meandering in and out as footmen, maids, and a few of her cousins carried in trunks and reticules and hat boxes. They had all come to Chalcroft, the family seat of the Fitzroys.

The crystal chandeliers and landscape paintings, which adorned the great hall, were as familiar to Olivia as each of the people below.

And it was Christmas once again. This year had welcomed new life into the Fitzroy family, and another gathering of the three brothers and their twelve daughters.

Well, not everyone. Olivia, the eldest of the Chalcroft sib-lings, watched as Joy and Harmony helped each other remove their pelisses, shaking the snow from their shoulders. They had come from Bath, not too far a distance—not as far as Esther, Lucy, and Jemima who had all traveled from London.

Not that it appeared to have exhausted them, however.

"Oh, Chalcroft, you never change," said Jemima with a heavy sigh. "If only Caroline could be here, she loves it at Christmas."

"She will give birth any moment, Jemmy, you know there was no possibility of her traveling," scolded their sister Esther. "Really, it's not all about you!"

"I did not say it was," Jemima retorted with the temper all the Fitzroys knew so well—but, she was prevented from getting into a real huff by the gentle hand of her husband on her shoulder.

Olivia watched, transfixed, as her cousin beamed up at Hugh, her shoulders immediately relaxing. What a strange thing it was, love. How transformative. How utterly all-consuming. No one had expected the fiery eldest London Fitzroy to marry at all, let alone to a soldier.

Cheeks hot, Olivia attempted to push the thought away. She was a woman now, not a child. She could leave behind all those silly thoughts of love and affection, which she had believed she shared with—

No. She would not think of him. That childhood fancy was one she was leaving firmly behind, she told herself severely. Besides, she had not seen him since Easter, and she had been sure then, for a moment, when he had touched her hand...

But no. He had not said anything; and she had not wanted him to. It was not as though she had waited all Easter for him to say something. Not as though she had wept as he had left, words unspoken which she had been sure he felt.

She certainly felt.

Olivia swallowed. But this was difficult; a true family celebrating, no interlopers. Almost the whole family was here, and the very least she could do was greet everyone.

Though her father appeared to be doing a fine job of it, in his way.

"Careful of the carpet!" Olivia's Papa looked anxiously around as muddy and snowy footprints were stamped around the place. "Leonora will not like it—and the butler, you know, very severe on me!"

"Dearest Uncle William, do not fret yourself," said Esther with a kiss on his cheek. He was the favorite uncle, Olivia knew, pride soaring into her heart for her papa. "We'll hardly make any mess at all, and—"

"Careful!"

The cry went out just after there was anything anyone could do, and laughter rang about the chaotic family as a footman dropped a trunk, which burst and splattered gifts wrapped in brown paper all over the floor.

"Mercy, save us from raining presents!" quipped Lucy, grabbing at one to read the label.

"Don't read those!" Jemima said, hurtling toward them.

"You can't stop me!"

"Lucy Fitzroy, put that down or I shall cut off all your labels and—"

"Is there one for me?" Joy, always one to tease, giggled as she watched Jemima chase Lucy around the hall. "Careful, Uncle William's rug!"

Olivia grinned. There was nothing like Chalcroft during the holidays. All the chaos and wonder of family, with all the festive joy of Christmas. Even her mother would not begrudge a little snow about the place to witness such merriment.

"What is going on?"

Looking up, Olivia saw her sister, Katarina, glaring down at the scene below with a frown.

It was strange; Katarina, or Kitty as she was known to her sisters, was usually one of the first to rush downstairs and welcome their Fitzroy cousins. An exuberant, fiery Fitzroy, she had more—it seemed—of her mother's Italian blood than their father's reliable English.

But today she had been reticent, almost dull at breakfast when their papa had told them today was the day that everyone arrived.

"Everyone's here," said Olivia with a smile. "At least, almost everyone. Caroline is giving birth apparently. Sophia stayed at home, her mother thought her too young this year, and I haven't seen Maria anywhere, have you?"

Their youngest sister, Maria, was a little shy with family still. Kitty shrugged.

"What does it matter to me? The same old people, the same old traditions."

Olivia's mouth fell open. "Some old people—Kitty, they are our cousins! And you love the Chalcroft Christmas traditions!"

Kitty shrugged again. There was certainly something odd about her, now Olivia came to think about it. She had not come to the kitchen to stir the Christmas pudding weeks ago, and though she had thought nothing of it at the time, it was unlike her.

"Are you feeling quite well?" she asked quietly. "It is not like you to—"

"It's just all so dull," said Kitty with a sigh. "I mean, when one has made a single Christmas wreath, has not one made them all?"

Olivia's mouth was still open, but as the hustle and bustle of embraces and catching up on news, and remarking on how well everyone looked continued below, she forced herself to close it.

Kitty did have these moods, of course. And it was strange, sometimes, having one's home invaded by all and sundry almost every Christmas. That was what happened when your father was the eldest of three brothers, and you lived at the seat of the family. Anyone could descend at any moment.

Olivia was the eldest, had the most comfort with it. Was more accustomed to being dragged in to entertain. Perhaps that was it.

"You don't have to go down," Olivia said gently. "If you do not wish to."

Kitty rolled her eyes. "Don't try to be like Mama, all noble. I know my duty, I know I must greet everyone. But still. Gowns and jewels and opera. It's all so dull."

There were some moments, Olivia thought darkly, and this was one of them, when she quite wondered how on earth she and Kitty were related, let alone sisters. Jewels? Opera? What on earth could be taken against such luxuries?

"Well, I am going to go down," said Olivia decidedly, rising to her feet. "It is only polite to—"

"Olivia! Is that you—you look marvelous!"

A smile crept across her face at the compliment paid her by one of her cousins, she could not tell who, but when Olivia looked around to say something to her sister, she was gone.

Well, she could not be expected to look after her siblings all the time. Being the eldest came with responsibility, true, but it should also come with excitement, and Olivia was determined to enjoy this festive season.

After all, what could prevent it?

"I am so glad you are all here safely," Olivia said with a broad smile, stepping as quickly and elegantly as she could down the wide staircase.

Her face fell slightly as she reached the bottom and saw just how differently attired she was to some of her cousins.

That was always the trouble, wasn't it? When one's family came to visit, one noticed the differences. Olivia knew that Chalcroft was an expensive home to maintain; she had heard her mother grumbling about it enough times to know that the roof always needed repairing, that sourcing enough coal for the fires was extortionate, and the number of servants one needed to maintain!

But it was only in moments like these that she noticed the stark difference. Joy and Harmony, her cousins from Bath, were adorned in the most delightful gowns in the latest fashions. Even Lucy, not one for fripperies, had a new gown on.

Olivia only knew this, of course, because their gowns had a delicate embroidery at the sleeves, which she had never seen before, and if there was any certainty in life, it was that the Bath Fitzroys were the height of fashion.

"Olivia!" Lucy rushed toward her and embraced her. "You're here! Of course you're here, you live here—did you help with the decorations? Did you know we were coming today? Am I sleeping in the Blue Room again?"

Olivia laughed, her cousin's many questions pouring from her like snow down from the heavens. That was always the way with her London cousins, always demanding information, always full of excitement.

"I am here, I did help with the decorations, I did know you were coming today, and I have no idea where you are sleeping," Olivia said with a laugh. "And wouldn't you like to remove your shoes and put on some slippers? I really do think our butler may be a little concerned if you tramp that mud about the place."

Lucy looked down, alarmed at her own feet. "Lord, I suppose you're right. Father, where are my slippers?"

Meandering away, Olivia was left alone to gaze at her chattering, enthusiastic family. The Bath Fitzroys had not seen the London Fitzroys for some time, so everyone was desperate to catch up with everyone else, and the place echoed with laughter and well wishes.

"Penny for your thoughts?"

Olivia smiled as her father put his arm around her shoulders, tightening his hand. "I am not sure they are worth a penny."

There was a twinkle in Papa's eyes. "Oh, I don't know."

Olivia sighed happily. "I was just thinking how pleasant it was for everyone to be here. All the family together—or at least, most of us. How enjoyable it is to be only family, just the Fitzroys."

Her father smiled, though there was something rather strange about his look that Olivia did not understand. Just as he opened his mouth to say something, there was a shriek.

"Oh, no!"

Olivia and her father looked around to see Esther raise her hands to her mouth.

"Esther, what on earth is the matter?" Jemima asked from where she stood by the fire.

Olivia was about to ask the same thing. Her cousin Esther looked absolutely horrified, and Lucy stepped toward her, placing a calming hand on her arm.

Her heart flickered painfully. Surely something terrible could not happen the moment that everyone arrived at Chalcroft for Christmas?

"Oh, I cannot believe it," said Esther. "I left my book at home!"

Murmured laughter echoed around the room as Esther's shoulders slumped.

"Dear me, you really had me worried there," said Isabella, Olivia's sister who laughed nervously. "But don't worry, Chalcroft's library will surely suit! Come, maybe we have a copy of your book."

The two women disappeared, and Hugh Rotherham, Jemima's husband, cleared his throat. "Perhaps we should all move to the drawing room? A little warmer, somewhere for some of us to sit down—"

"I am perfectly well," Jemima said—a little too quickly, in Olivia's opinion. Jemima was not the delicate sort, why did she need to rest? "But I suppose I could sit down. For a moment," she added as her husband smiled at her.

"We'll come, too," said Lucy, pulling at Joy's hand. "Where's Maria? Still hiding from us?"

The chattering mass started to move slowly toward the drawing room, and Olivia sighed happily.

"As I said," she murmured in a low voice to her father with a mischievous grin on her face. "Nothing like family."

But Papa did not smile back. As the great hall started to clear, it became more and more obvious that he had not responded— and only then did a terrible thought cross Olivia's mind.

"You...you did not invite anyone else for Christmas, did you, Papa?"

His hesitation was more than enough to tell her that was precisely what he had done.

"Papa, you promised a family Christmas!"

"And that is exactly what you will have," her Papa said quickly, releasing her shoulder to step before her with a calming expression. "After all the hubbub of three Fitzroy weddings two years ago, I agreed, a nice, quiet, family Christmas was precisely what we needed. Why do you think I invited everyone to Chalcroft?"

Olivia looked warily at her father. If she had been Maria's age, she would have left it at that. "But...?"

William Fitzroy hesitated. "But...well, it would hardly be kind to leave out people we knew and loved who were practically family. Especially if they were going to be alone, at...at Christmas."

A knot formed in Olivia's stomach.

"You didn't," she breathed.

"And I thought, well, he would be alone otherwise, wouldn't he?" said her father in a rapidly rising voice. "And no one should be alone at Christmas, it's the most festive time of year, isn't it?"

Heat was starting to rise in Olivia's body. Her father had not said the exact words, not revealed to her who he had invited, but she was not sure he needed to. She knew precisely what he had done, and as shame and embarrassment flushed through her, Olivia knew this was going to be absolutely the worst Christmas she had ever suffered.

Why would he do it? Why would her father, knowing that she wished for nothing but a calm and quiet Christmas, do this to her?

Why would he invite *him* of all people?

A memory shot through her... A Christmas when she had been a child, perhaps eight or nine. Isabella had been teasing her, and she had hidden in the kitchen, the servants leaving her be.

And he had come. He had come to cheer her up, that mischievous smile always able to make her laugh.

She was not laughing now.

"I asked for a quiet Christmas," Olivia said in a low voice.

Her words were rather unpleasantly interrupted by loud, raucous laughter from the drawing room. Isabella appeared to be telling a story to the family, something she was marvelous at. She was always able to hold the attention of a room.

"That does not disprove my point," said Olivia, glaring at her father as he remained silent. "Oh, how could you, Papa?"

"I would hope that if my child was alone, without parents, without siblings, that someone would welcome them into their home at Christmas time," said her father with a wry smile. "You are fortunate, Olivia. You have reached maturity with two parents still living, three sisters, and nine cousins, but Luke—"

Just hearing his name was enough to make Olivia's heart contract.

Luke. Luke Kingsley. He was coming here, then. Just when she had thought she would at least be able to relax with her cousins, not have to worry about anything, really put her feet up...

And Luke Kingsley would be here. At Chalcroft. For Christmas.

"—has no parents, no family," her papa continued, not noticing the sudden wrench of agony which had seared his daughter. "And that is why I invited him, Olivia. Not to hurt you. Besides, I thought you liked Luke? He is almost a part of the family. He and his father came here so often when you were children."

Olivia smiled painfully as her stomach lurched. "Almost part of the family, yes. But not quite."

Not how she wanted. She could think the words, even if she could not say them. Not quite her family, although for the last few years whenever she had looked at Luke Kingsley, she had hoped. Wondered. Thought what it would be like for him to be part of her family. To be her family.

It had been different when they were children, of course. Running about Chalcroft, playing in the music room, exploring the gun room as though it was a far-off civilization.

And when they were a little older, riding out in the parkland, exploring Chalcroft Farm, racing each other for pennies.

And that was when it had happened. One day, a few years ago, they had been riding and Olivia had looked over at Luke, who was laughing, and a jolt of desire had struck her heart, and

EMILY E K MURDOCH

that had been it.

The boy who had been her companion in the summers, and some Christmases, was no longer merely the boy who came to visit. He was...everything. He was Luke. He was hers, even if he did not know it.

Olivia shook her head slightly, as though that would dislodge the thought, but it had crept into her heart already. Had done years ago, if she could admit it to herself.

A passing fancy. A fancy, that was all. It did not mean anything.

It meant nothing that she found his face the kindest, the most handsome.

It meant nothing that his company was what she sought whenever he was visiting.

It meant nothing that the last time he visited, he had passed her a book, and their fingers had touched, Olivia had felt...felt everything. Heat and cold and joy and hatred, hatred at herself for loving him.

Olivia swallowed. She did not love Luke Kingsley. He was the son of her father's best friend, that was all. Part of the family, she supposed. As close as anyone could be to them, without being a Fitzroy.

And she was absolutely, equivocally, definitely not in love with him.

"Olivia?"

Olivia blinked. Her father was looking at her, concern spreading across his face.

"I miscalculated, didn't I?" he said heavily. "That is the trouble with daughters, and I have plenty of them. I never quite get it right. I am sorry, Olivia, if I had known you were so against the boy—"

"I'm not," cut in Olivia, then hated herself for it. "Besides, he's not a boy."

Papa snorted. "I suppose he is not. Well, it is too late now, I am afraid, to rescind the invitation. You will just have to suffer his presence, if that is not too much to ask."

Olivia looked up into her father's face, and the embarrassment of loving Luke Kingsley, a gentleman who saw her as just
one of a myriad of Fitzroy sisters and nothing more, was eclipsed
by the shame of disappointing her father.

What did he ask of her? That she be civil. Kitty may struggle
with such a task, but she would not. She would not let him down.

Besides, it was a few days before Christmas Day. She had
enough time to reconcile with the idea that he would be arriving,
disturbing her peace.

"Fine, Papa," Olivia said with not nearly as much grace as she
had hoped. "I suppose I can put up with him for a few days—and
I suppose it is not too much to ask, to have one interloper."

"Interloper? Goodness, who is that?"

Olivia froze. It could not be. She had imagined it; imagined
the words, heard them in Luke Kingsley's tone merely because
she was thinking about him.

But as she turned slowly to the front door, it was to see a
gentleman standing there in traveling greatcoat, top hat, and the
most irritatingly charming smile she had ever beheld.

"Kingsley!" Papa roared, stepping away from her to greet his
guest. "Dear Lord, I was so absorbed in speaking to Olivia I did
not even hear the door open! How are you, the roads were kind
to you?"

Olivia swallowed down the panic rising in her heart as she
stared not at Luke Kingsley, but at his boots.

He was here.

Luke Kingsley was here, and would be spending all of
Christmas with them.

Luke Kingsley was here because he had nowhere else to go,
and her father was kind. That was all.

She should certainly not be getting any ideas into her head
about him. About his kindness, his soft hands—hands that she
wanted to touch her again. Take her hand, and kiss—

"Olivia?"

Olivia blinked. Both her father and Luke were staring at her.

"I beg your pardon?" she managed to say, voice hoarse as though she had run a thousand miles. Her heart was certainly beating quickly enough.

"I said," repeated Luke with a mischievous smile, removing his top hat and allowing a curl of hair to fall over his face. "I hope we shall have a merry time of it?"

Olivia swallowed. "Oh. Oh yes. A very merry time, I am sure."

CHAPTER TWO

O LIVIA HAD MADE herself three very firm promises when she was dressing for dinner.

Firstly, she was being a fool, and she was not going to act the fool any longer. She was Miss Olivia Fitzroy. She was the eldest daughter of the eldest Fitzroy brother. She could be elegance personified, if she concentrated. She did not have to allow herself to be embarrassed.

Secondly, so far no one appeared to have noticed she was utterly thrown by the appearance of Luke Kingsley, and she was going to do her utmost to ensure it stayed that way. No one could know how her heart fluttered painfully whenever she looked at him, or that his broad shoulders did something strange to her insides. Especially not Luke himself.

And thirdly—

"Olivia, have you seen my diamond earbobs?"

Olivia blinked. Her bedchamber door was open, and her sister Isabella was standing there, gown on but unbuttoned, with a look of panic in her eyes. They were sharing a bedchamber while their guests were here, but her sister had rushed back to her room to look for her jewelry.

Jewelry, it appeared, she had not found.

"What?" Olivia said stupidly. She had been so lost in her looking glass, telling herself precisely how she was not going to embarrass herself today, that she had entirely ignored the sound of the door opening.

Isabella sighed. "What is wrong with you? Ever since everyone arrived, you have been so strange. Distant. Not like you at all."

Olivia swallowed. "No, I haven't."

"Yes, you have."

"No, I haven't," said Olivia as firmly as she could muster. She would not be drawn into a debate on this. "And I haven't seen your diamond earbobs. Borrow Maria's."

Isabella rolled her eyes. "Maria said to borrow yours."

Olivia could not help but smile at this. It was so like Isabella and Maria to get into a tangle over jewelry. It was a miracle they could ever find any when it came to dressing for dinner.

"You're wearing a brooch."

Olivia looked down self-consciously at the little pearl and gold brooch she had attached to the front of her gown. "You don't like it?"

"You never wear brooches," frowned Isabella. "You never wear much jewelry at all, but never a brooch. Why are you wearing something so pretty?"

"You should hurry up," said Olivia, her throat dry. "You're not even dressed properly, and the dinner gong will be going any moment."

"But my diamond earbobs!" wailed Isabella in a teasing tone, a mischievous grin on her face. "Maria said to borrow yours, and you're wearing yours!"

"Then borrow Katarina's."

That was always the benefit of being one of four sisters. There was always someone else you could borrow from. Olivia smiled wryly to herself. She could hardly imagine what it was like being a London Fitzroy; there were six of them.

Isabella sighed. "I suppose I will have to. I haven't seen her in hours, and she's not in her bedchamber, so I'll just take them."

"No, don't do—"

But Isabella was gone before Olivia could tell her absolutely not to just take her sister's diamond earbobs—which, now she came to think of it, was probably precisely why Isabella's were missing in the first place.

A slow smile crept across her face. Even with the sudden arrival of Luke Kingsley throwing her off balance, Olivia knew she could always depend on her sisters to be utterly ridiculous.

Taking a deep breath, she turned back to the looking glass. A woman with dark hair, dark eyes, a brooch, and a furious expression looked back at her.

Olivia laughed, despite herself. Well, if she went downstairs for dinner like this, everyone was certain to know that there was something amiss. The very least she could do was attempt to remain calm.

Calm. That was all she needed. Not to permit her heart to race wildly whenever she saw him. Not to drift toward him whenever he was speaking, just to hear his voice. Not to imagine what it would be like if he told her, in low tones, that he loved her…

Olivia sighed, and took off the pearl and gold brooch, laying it carefully back down on her toilette table. If Isabella was going to notice such a thing while in the middle of a catastrophe—for that was surely how her sister would describe not being able to find diamond earbobs—everyone else would surely notice her efforts to impress.

And so would *he*.

She could never think of him as just Kingsley; that was his father, a pleasant man whose sudden death had been a shock to them all. She certainly could not call him Luke! At least, not to his face. Not in public, before others. Olivia's cheeks flushed at the mere thought.

So, he was Luke Kingsley in her mind. She would not speak to him while he was visiting this Christmas, so she never had to worry about how to address him.

Olivia swallowed, her shoulders slumped, and remained

staring at her reflection until the gong went.

"I'm not ready!"

"Is that the gong?"

"Does anyone know where my sash is? My blue sash?"

"You mean *my* sash?"

Olivia smiled as she opened her bedchamber door. The corridor was filled with the hubbub of nine ladies getting ready for dinner. Even with family, one dressed for dinner, and so of course absolute chaos ensued.

A lady's maid rushed, harried, from one bedchamber to another. "Here's your sash, Miss—"

"That is my sash!"

"Are you the only Fitzroy ready?"

Olivia looked up, her feet unable to move. Luke Kingsley was standing on the landing, dressed in a painfully dashing jacket with a blue silk cravat tied in a complex knot, a wry smile on his face.

Olivia tried to smile. Luke Kingsley had known her and her sisters for years, she told herself sternly. There was absolutely nothing strange in him being here. He was her father's guest, and she had told her father she would be polite.

Polite. What did that mean when one was staring into the eyes of the man you loved? A man who so clearly did not return those affections, but only sought to tease her?

"Ready?" said Olivia in a strange gargle.

Luke's brow furrowed. "Yes, ready. Are you the only one besides myself?"

Olivia was not sure whether she had enough presence of mind to speak, but fortunately was prevented from needing to by the sudden appearance of Lucy in her undershift.

Her scream echoed down the corridor at the sight of a gentleman looking at her when she was so indecorously undressed, and the shrieks of laughter from all her sisters and cousins as they peered out of their bedchambers to see what all the fuss was about caused a cacophony of sound.

Olivia laughed, too, grateful for the distraction. Lucy rushed down the corridor, and Luke continued to laugh. In that time, she was able to pull herself together.

She was no fool, no chit of fourteen who had no idea how to conduct herself in public. She was a Fitzroy, and she was not going to be overcome by a mere man.

Probably.

"Yes, it appears I am the first ready to descend," Olivia said as calmly as she could manage, now Lucy had disappeared.

"Shall we go down?"

Shall we go down. Such innocent words, but Olivia found her stomach lurch. *We.* There was no we between herself and Luke, even if she wanted there to be.

"Capital idea," she said brightly, as though he were one of her sisters, trying to ignore the chiseled jaw and the way his eyes sparkled as she spoke. "Shall we?"

Olivia had taken a step toward the staircase before she realized what had happened. A hand on her arm. A strong man's hand. One that made her skin tingle, that shot waves of something she did not understand through her body.

"Allow me," said Luke quietly.

Olivia looked up at him. He was so tall; was he taller than the last time he had visited? She could not remember. He certainly felt tall now, as he carefully placed her hand in the crook of his arm before walking slowly with her to the staircase.

If she was not careful, Olivia knew, she was going to faint. Which was ridiculous. She was not a girl in a fairytale; this was real life, and Luke was just a man.

A man holding her arm in his. A man gently stepping down the sweeping staircase, the banister entwined with holly and ivy. A man who she wished to walk beside the rest of her life.

That was all.

Olivia swallowed, her foot fumbling slightly on the following step. She tightened her grip on Luke's arm instinctively, leaning on him for support, and he held her. His strength settled her, and Olivia found herself glancing up once again at the gentleman she knew so well, and had adored for so long.

"I must say, Chalcroft looks beautiful at this time of year," he murmured quietly as they reached the bottom of the staircase.

Olivia laughed like a fool. "Yes—yes, Chalcroft does look beautiful."

Luke glanced at her. "Very beautiful."

Why did her cheeks have to betray her so utterly as he spoke those words? Despite knowing full well that Luke was speaking of her home and not herself, Olivia could not help it. A rush of warmth spread throughout her body.

Would he notice? Did he see the effect he had on her?

After all these years of knowing each other, could he sense that something had changed, at least for her?

"Olivia," Luke said quietly.

Olivia pulled her arm away. "Thank you, Mr. Kingsley, that was very kind of—"

"It's Lord Kingsley, actually."

Olivia blinked. They were alone in the hall, thank goodness, so there was no one else but Luke to see her make an entire fool of herself. "I beg your pardon?"

There was a wry smile on his face, setting off his handsome jaw perfectly. "Lord Kingsley. Now my father is gone, I inherited the title."

There was only one thing that Luke Kingsley needed to be absolutely perfect, and that was a title. Damn.

How was she going to survive this Christmas with such a handsome, charming, and now titled gentleman in the place— one she had cared about a little too deeply for a little too long?

"Right," she said as briskly as she could manage. "Yes. Well. Lord Kingsley. Fine. Dining room. Yes."

Without waiting for him to respond—as though he could respond to such nonsense—Olivia turned on her heels and marched toward the dining room. Surely there would be other people there—her parents, her uncles. Anyone who could rid her of this strange attention that she was managing to draw to herself.

As she entered the dining room, she saw to her relief that she was right. Her mother, Leonora Fitzroy, was speaking with the butler while Uncle Rupert and Uncle Arthur admired the place settings.

"Ah, Olivia, you do not surprise me by being the first down," said her mother. "And Luke, too, how wonderful. I have placed you two together in fact, right here."

Together.

Olivia glared at her mother. This was the trouble of keeping such ridiculous passions to oneself, she told herself silently. If she had ever deigned to let her mother know that she harbored this…this fancy for Luke, for that was all it was, a fancy, then her mother would never have done this idiotic, cruel—

"Wonderful, that is precisely who I would have asked to be seated beside," said Luke smoothly as he entered the room, bowing to her mother.

Olivia smiled weakly. "Wonderful."

And it would have been, if Luke returned even a smidgen of her affection. But he was the same old Luke, same teasing air, same interest in spending time with her, his childhood companion. And that was all.

He saw her as nothing more than one in a million Fitzroys— which was unfair, because there were only twelve of them.

Olivia tried to think swiftly, but there was something rather disobligingly preventing her from thinking clearly at all.

Luke was standing right beside her. She could sense his presence, feel how close he was. And she would have to endure being seated beside him? All dinner?

"Surely Mr.—Lord Kingsley would prefer to be near Papa," Olivia tried hopefully as her sisters Isabella and Maria entered the room with a few cousins. "Or—"

"Olivia Fitzroy, when you have your own home and own establishment, then you can decide on the seating arrangements," her mother said impressively, that Italian boldness her daughters knew all too well coming to the fore. "And not before! Now sit!"

Olivia knew there was no point in attempting to argue with her mother. Leonora Fitzroy had given each of her daughters her Italian spirit, and though they frequently had blazing rows—instantly forgotten in a moment, naturally—they knew better than to argue with her before their guests.

One guest, in particular, looked a little piqued. "I promise, Miss Olivia, I should be sufficient company. I promise to be an excellent conversationalist."

Olivia tried to smile. It was not Luke's conversational skills that was the problem, but she could hardly say that, could she? Declaring her puppy love to a man she now knew was a viscount would hardly endear herself to her family, and as to Luke...

She glanced up at the tall gentleman, who was now engaging some of her cousins in a lively debate about the correct lyrics to a Christmas carol.

If only he wasn't so charming. If only she could rid herself of this dependency on him, on this desire to be close to him...

"Come, sit!" Her father had entered the room and spread out his arms wide, inviting his guests to find their seats. "My wonderful wife has taken the time to write little name cards for us all, so find your place and enjoy the food. Wine, Arthur?"

As Olivia's father poured wine for one of his brothers, she stepped forward and tried to find the little name card her mother had written in her large, expressive handwriting.

She found Luke's first, of course. A little lurch in her stomach pained her as she saw the way her mother had curled the L. And beside it, her own.

"Let me draw out your chair, Olivia," said Luke's voice from just behind her.

"Oh," said Olivia, heat splashing across her chest. He had always called her Olivia when they were children, why did it feel so strange now? "Thank you."

Luke had to come incredibly close to her as he pulled out the chair and slowly pushed it in as she sat. Olivia felt his breath on her neck and shivered.

There was something so intimate about it. So precious. So personal.

"And here, let me help you, Isabella," said Luke jovially, helping Isabella sit on the other side of Olivia.

Olivia's smile, one she had not realized she was wearing, disappeared.

She was a fool. She had thought for a moment, a fleeting, glorious moment, that she had been something special. Someone special to Luke, but it was mere politeness, that was all.

The last thing she should do was convince herself that she was anymore but a...a person. A Fitzroy. That was all. Luke saw not her curves, her lips, the way she looked at him. The way she wanted to be looked at by him.

"—and I am pleased to announce," said her Uncle Arthur loudly, his words cutting through her thoughts, "that Caroline has been safely delivered of her baby!"

Cries of delight rang out around the dining room, Esther's eyes shining, Lucy clapping her hands together, Jemima smiling wryly at her husband, and even Isabella looked delighted.

"Congratulations, Grandfather," said Olivia's papa with a short laugh. "Quite healthy, I hope?"

"Little James appears to be doing quite well," said Uncle Arthur, his chest puffing out proudly. "The Viscount Cheshire, the moment of his birth! When I return to London..."

"So, tell me," said Luke as he sat beside her and dropped his napkin on his lap. "Chalcroft. Is it much changed this last year? I admit, I was sorry not to visit sooner, but then so much of my time has been taken up with my own estate that I have not had the time for visiting."

Olivia swallowed. Speaking to Luke, having his full attention as the footmen brought in the dishes and the genial chatter of her family grew around them, was something she had craved in the past. His full attention, it was so precious.

But she could not permit herself to be dazzled by it now. Luke's charms, such as they were, were not designed for her and her alone.

They were the practiced art of a gentleman, Olivia knew that—and now he had risen to the rank of viscount, he would undoubtedly be practicing on her. Practicing for when he met a lady he wished to entertain, to woo, to propose marriage to. Her stomach contracted painfully.

Yes, that was it. And she would not permit herself to be merely someone's practice.

"No," Olivia said coldly. "Not much has changed."

Luke nodded, as though expecting her to say more. When she lapsed into silence, he continued, "I think you would really like Kingsley Hall. 'Tis not as extensive in its grounds as Chalcroft, of course, but the house is really rather fine. Would…would you like to visit one day?"

Yes, of course, Olivia's heart cried. If only it were a true invitation, one spoken from affection. One that was a preempt to love. Not a mere formality.

"No," said Olivia quietly, dropping her gaze to her plate. "No, I would not."

An awkward silence arose between them. From the corner of her eye, Olivia could see a slight flush on Luke's cheeks. He was ashamed of her impertinence, and well he should be. Olivia was certain that if either of her parents could hear her rudeness, they would be mortified.

She was a little mortified herself.

"Well." Luke seemed desirous of saying something, but did not appear to know what.

Olivia picked up her knife and fork for the want of something to do, and picked at the fried sole which had been brought through. Though the recipe was one she knew well, and liked, the flaked fish tasted dry in her mouth.

This was agony. How long would she be forced to sit here beside the man that she knew she loved, when all she could do was treat him ill?

"And are you…are you excited about Christmas?" Luke attempted.

Olivia sipped her wine to give herself a few moments to think about her response, but all she could manage was. "No."

"No?"

"Ouch!" Olivia rubbed her side and turned away from Luke to her cousin Esther, who had apparently swapped seats with Isabella, risking Leonora's anger. "What was that for?"

Her hiss was low enough, Olivia hoped, to prevent Luke from hearing her. What had provoked Esther to give her such a sharp elbow?

"You are being rude," said Esther firmly in a low voice, glancing at Luke. "What has the gentleman done to offend you?"

"I'm not being rude," Olivia said with a flush that immediately betrayed her. "I...I am just quiet, that is all."

"Nonsense," said Esther firmly. "I have never heard such nonsense in my life, and I live with Lucy. Besides, it's Luke! We saw enough of him on visits to Chalcroft, he is practically family, and he has spent far more time with you. What has he done? What ails you? What has got into you, Olivia? You were perfectly fine when we arrived."

She certainly had been, Olivia thought sadly. And then Luke Kingsley had arrived, and taken with him all her serenity.

It was impossible to be polite to a gentleman who only teased her heart the more with every word.

"Concentrate on your own food," snapped Olivia at Esther's continued prodding, "and let me converse as I see fit."

"I hope everything is well?" Luke peered over at them, and Olivia felt hot as he leaned closer to join the hastily whispered conversation she was having with her cousin.

"I was just saying," began Esther, causing Olivia's blood to run cold, but thankfully her father interrupted by tapping a glass to gain the attention of everyone in the room.

"If I may say a small something," said Olivia's papa as he rose. There was raucous laughter.

"As long as it's only one thing, Uncle William," chortled Joy.

"Joy Fitzroy!"

"I promise it will only be the one," said William with a grin, "though I cannot promise you will all like it. I know for certain that Katarina here will be most displeased."

He smiled at his middle daughter, clearly in the hope that she would find his comment amusing, but Olivia could see, even from the other end of the table, that it had not gone down well.

"What do you mean by that?"

"I just meant," their Papa said quickly, "that I wanted to make a short announcement. As we are all together, at least most of us, and it has been such a long time since so many Fitzroys have been, I have organized a little entertainment for us."

"A ball!" Lucy burst out.

Her uncle grinned. "How on earth did you guess?"

There were gasps of excitement up and down the table, and Olivia felt her heart sink just as her cousins and sisters' exhilaration rose. A ball. With Luke at Chalcroft?

"Goodness," said Hugh with a grin. "What have we done to deserve this?"

"It is our own fault, I suppose," Harmony's husband David quipped. "We were foolish enough to marry into this madness!"

Both of their wives tapped them on the shoulder in mock outrage as giggles erupted from the younger girls.

"Christmas Eve," pronounced Papa proudly. "I have invited a few of the local gentlemen to make up our numbers—after all, with our nine ladies dancing, they will need partners! And I hope you will oblige, young Kingsley."

Luke nodded, and Olivia felt her heart skip a beat as he said quietly, "Of course, Mr. Fitzroy. I will endeavor to please."

CHAPTER THREE

"**B**UT YOU HAVE always loved wreath making!"

Olivia smiled as cheerfully as she could muster as she looked up from the sofa at her cousin Harmony, a confused expression on her face.

"I know," Olivia said. "And I enjoyed it last year, and the year before, and countless years before that. And I do not want to do it this year."

They were in the library, of course. Olivia had discovered in the two days since Luke had arrived at Chalcroft that for some reason, this was one of the few places he rarely entered. It was strange; she had always recalled Luke as being a widely read man, but she did not waste too much time worrying about it.

It could not be that he was avoiding her. Or perhaps it was. Olivia could hardly tell whether he was following her merrily because he saw her as nothing more than one of many Fitzroys, or avoiding her because she was dull.

The point was, she had found a place that was not her bedchamber—too likely to draw attention, and besides, she was forced to share it with Isabella—that she could reasonably hope to avoid Luke for another hour.

Avoid the way his glance made her skin tingle.

Avoid the way his presence made her warm, even without saying a word.

Avoid the thoughts that raced through her mind, thoughts that young ladies were certainly not supposed to think about gentlemen...

"But you love wreath making!" Harmony repeated, standing beside the sofa with a wire frame in her hands. "You love it!"

Olivia sighed. That was the trouble with being a part of a family like the Fitzroys. From the little she had heard from others at the school she and her sisters had attended, there were some families who were hardly involved in each other's lives, who did not pay any attention to what one or the other was doing, and actually did not enjoy the company of each other!

It had been strange to hear, and Olivia had always felt glad of the closeness of the Fitzroy family she loved so dearly.

In and out of each other's pockets, it had been mere days after Jemima, Caroline, and Harmony's engagements that the entire Fitzroy family had been informed. And Olivia had loved that. Loved their inability to do anything without the whole family knowing.

Until now, that was. How irritating for Harmony to remember so well just how much she had always enjoyed wreath making.

The choosing of the foliage, the careful way one had to wind it around the wire, the pleasure of selecting certain ribbons or other adornments to complete it...

Chalcroft's many doors were usually festooned with wreaths by the time Olivia had wearied of the craft. But not this year. This year, the Chalcroft Fitzroys had put off their wreath making so that all the Fitzroy cousins could do it together.

Olivia had been stern with herself, despite her better judgement. Any activity which could bring her into closer proximity with Luke—with Lord Kingsley—was one she absolutely had to avoid.

Even if it made her miserable in the process. Even if it was drawing, despite her best efforts, even more attention.

"I said, I do not wish to make wreaths," Olivia said to the

hovering Harmony.

"But—"

"What's all this fuss?" Joy, Harmony's sister, stepped into the room, evidently having overheard the noise.

Olivia tried to calm her breathing as she looked away from her cousins and at the book she had randomly picked from the shelves when she had heard someone approach. Her attempt to hide behind it, to prevent anyone from speaking to her, had utterly failed.

She blinked. She had found a book on anatomy. Elegant engravings of animal skeletons covered the pages. Dear Lord...

"Olivia—*Olivia*—says she will not be partaking in wreath making this year," said Harmony with great emphasis.

"Nonsense," said Joy cheerfully. "I am sure she merely wishes to give us visitors enough time to play with it ourselves, before she sweeps in and makes improvements."

Olivia could not help a wry smile. "While that is an excellent idea for some of your designs are most grievous to the eye—*no*. I simply do not want to make a wreath."

Joy's grin started to fade as silence crept up on them. "You...you are in earnest? I thought this merely a jest to tease Harmony."

"Why would she do that?" Harmony said hotly.

Olivia raised a hand. "Peace! If I had realized my absence from wreath making would have caused such a fuss, I would have gone for a ride to ensure I was not even here!"

It was an excellent idea, now she came to think of it. Olivia glanced at the window. The snow had settled, as it always did at Chalcroft around this time of year, but that was nothing to her mare. Perhaps the cleverest idea was to go and saddle up her horse, and—

"Come on you three, are you not going to the gun room for wreath making?"

All three ladies looked up to see a handsome gentleman standing in the doorway. Luke's gaze moved between them, resting—at least to Olivia's eye—on her for a fraction longer than either of her cousins.

Which was foolishness. Wishful thinking. Pathetic thinking! *You believe Luke Kingsley has any interest in you?*

Would he not have said something? Would he not have made his intentions known, if he had any at all?

"Olivia," said Harmony in a sorrowful voice, "is not coming."

Now Luke's gaze was resting on her. Olivia tried not to let her discomfort show, though every inch of her skin prickled with the weight of his attention.

How did he do that? It was most unfair. Olivia was certain no one felt this uncomfortable, this warm, this strange in their own skin when she looked at them. It was Luke, and Luke alone, who had this power. This power over her. This power that made her want to—

"Not going to make a wreath?" asked Luke quietly, his face falling. "I have heard so much about this Fitzroy Christmas tradition, and everyone says that you are by far the best at it, Olivia. I am usually here too late to partake, but I thought this year—well. You are the best, Olivia."

Joy and Harmony looked at Olivia, one with triumph, the other with an 'I told you so' expression that was most unbecoming.

Olivia swallowed. *You are the best, Olivia.* If only he was not saying that about her wreath making but about…about her.

But she pushed the thought aside. This was her own home, for goodness' sake! It was ridiculous that she was going to be strong-armed into doing something that she had no wish to, merely because that was the way it was always done.

Even if Luke had always been the one to egg her on when they were younger. Even if it was his fault that a fence had to be put up around the fishpond in the village because he had dared her to swim in it.

Olivia felt a flush rush through her body. She had stripped off her gown without a second thought then. Luke had taken off his shirt and jumped in after her. The innocence of childhood, but they had not been children then, had they? Near fifteen.

Yet she had felt no shame. Luke had been as one of her sisters. He was far more than that now, if only he knew it.

"And besides," said Luke with a glint in his eyes that was all the more charming now that Olivia had noticed it, "I have never made a wreath before. I was rather hoping that you would be able to take some time out of your own creation to help me with mine."

Olivia swallowed. This was all most unfair. All she wished was to avoid the company of a gentleman who made her want to rip all her clothes off and kiss him.

Was that truly too much to ask?

Pushing the thought far down into her soul, where hopefully no one—including herself—would ever find it again, Olivia forced herself to look down at her book.

"I said I was not going to be making a wreath," she said as strongly as she could muster. Her eyes flickered over the skull of a fox. "I do not see what difference that makes to anyone else. I am not stopping anyone from making a wreath. There are plenty of people who know how to do it."

She would not look up. She would not permit herself the joy or terror of seeing how her words hurt—or made no difference at all—to Luke's expression.

"I had better see where my David has got to," said Harmony vaguely as she drifted away.

Her sister Joy followed her with a laugh. "Don't be ridiculous—you are just on the hunt for the pianoforte, aren't you? I saw Uncle William has moved it. How long has it been since you played…"

Their voices disappeared. Silence fell once again on the library, and Olivia breathed a sigh of relief. Finally, she had been left alone.

"I really would appreciate your help with the wreaths."

Olivia dropped her book. In the bustle of her cousins' departure, she had neither noticed nor heard Luke step away from the doorframe and into the library.

But he had. He was standing right before her, his eyes pleading, as though his very life would end if Olivia did not stir herself to help him make a wreath.

It twisted her heart to see him like that. If only Luke was pleading for a kiss, or her hand in marriage, or something far more delightful that Olivia was certain she should not be thinking about.

But no. It was about wreaths. Christmas wreaths, of all things!

"Did my mother put you up to this?" Olivia asked suspiciously.

Luke chuckled at her words. "You think I need to be bribed to spend time with you? Come now, how many times as children did we play about and make things?"

Thousands of times, Olivia wanted to say. *And each time I felt honored, somehow, that you had chosen me as a playmate from my four sisters. Every time I worried that it would be the last time, and then suddenly it was, because you were a man and I was almost a lady, and somewhere the childish nature of our games had disappeared. Disappeared into something far more interesting.*

And, of course, I want to make a wreath with you. I would do anything for you.

Olivia bit back the temptation to say one, or all of these things, and smiled painfully. "Wreaths are not that difficult."

Luke extended a hand. "Show me."

She was left, really, with absolutely no choice. Olivia knew it, Luke knew it—perhaps that was why there was a teasing smile on his face. There could be no other reason.

"Well," Olivia said awkwardly, ignoring Luke's offered hand, though her eyes were continually drawn to it as she stood up, "we should go on to the…the…gun room."

Had Luke been this close to the sofa when she had been sitting on it? Olivia was not sure. All she knew now was that standing, Luke was right beside her, inches from her, her breath catching in her throat as she attempted not to notice the warmth of his body so close to hers.

Olivia tilted her head up. His lips were mere inches from hers. If she was bold, if she had any indication Luke felt more for her than the sisterly affection he showed every Fitzroy, she would kiss him. Would taste the pleasure of—

"Olivia?"

Olivia blinked. "Gun room. Yes."

Stepping away from him was one of the most difficult things she had ever done, but somehow, she managed it. The gun room was on the other side of the house, and Chalcroft was large, giving Olivia plenty of time—or so she thought—to calm herself before she had to be in the presence of the rest of the family.

As it was…

"You appear a little warm, Olivia," said Luke calmly, easily keeping pace with her as she strode at almost breakneck speed along the corridors.

Damn these cheeks of hers! Why couldn't they just behave themselves, that's what she wanted to know!

"Nonsense," said Olivia quietly. "I just—ah, here we are."

She had never before been so relieved to find herself in the loud bustle of her family, or to lose the precious companionship of Luke and Luke alone—but this was starting to become too much.

Her thoughts, her emotions, her wild desires, they had always been contained with Luke as an idea, a gentleman far away who she could not see, or touch, or smell. His visits had become infrequent as he had become a man, and when his father died, they had stopped altogether.

But now…

Now he was here. Luke stood beside her, laughing openly at the antics of her cousins as Maria and Isabella attempted to surreptitiously place some holly in Jemima's hair, and Olivia could not bear it.

Luke's presence…it was too much. Intoxicating, preventing her from thinking, at times preventing her from speaking.

And the ball was still to come. She had dreamed of dancing with Luke, once, a dream she had transformed into a daydream whenever the skies were gray and there was nothing interesting to do.

But now that dream—or that nightmare, depending on the mood Olivia was in—could come to life. The Christmas Eve ball her father had organized, Luke would be here. And there was nothing she could do to quell the desire not only in her heart, but elsewhere…

"So," said a voice far too close to her ear for comfort. "Where do we start?"

Olivia stepped hastily away from the warm and inviting tones of Luke Kingsley. "Start?"

He gestured to the trestle tables that had been put up in the gun room, every inch covered in holly, ivy, greenery from the gardens, ribbons, bows, and even a few reels of gold and silver thread.

"The wreaths."

"The wreaths," repeated Olivia stupidly.

How could she say anything else? She was far too busy getting entirely lost in those eyes; eyes that seemed to pull her closer, so her feet almost tricked her into falling into his arms.

Olivia cleared her throat. If she wasn't going to make a total fool out of herself, she needed to get a grip on her behavior and stop staring into the eyes of a certain gentleman who was absolutely not interested in her.

How long was this foolishness, *her* foolishness, to continue?

"Wreaths," she said firmly. "Yes. Well, first you'll need to find a wire frame…"

One of the gardeners spent some time every year preparing the wire frames, once Maria proved the girls could not be trusted by spearing her finger and drawing blood a few years ago.

Olivia spotted one that was free, grabbed it, and thrust it into

Luke's waiting hands. "There you go. Now stick greenery into it. Simple."

She had just about managed to turn away before a hand grasped her arm. She could attempt to pull free; if it had been anyone else, particularly one of her sisters, Olivia would have done so.

But the grip of Luke was strong. Firm. Determined. Warm.

Olivia turned slowly to look at the man who appeared to be making her life a living hell. "What?"

Luke lifted up the wire frame. "Show me?"

Reluctant was hardly the word, Olivia thought savagely. Could she be more plain? Why wasn't he put off by this? Why was his strange attempt at civility not crushed by her obvious disdain? Where had all the ease gone between them?

It disappeared the moment you realized that you wanted to take off your gown again with Luke, but for an entirely different reason.

Olivia had to smile weakly. Disdain. An emotion so far removed from how she actually felt about Luke, it was almost laughable.

"One of my sisters can surely show you," Olivia tried to say, but only half the words escaped her lips before Luke closed the gap between them.

Olivia could see out of the corner of her eye that Isabella was watching her curiously—and were Joy and Harmony discussing her, as they whispered in the corner there?

"I am sure they all could show me, and would be perfectly adequate," said Luke in an undertone so that only she could hear him. It was strange, this sensation of closeness he created by the mere volume of his voice. Olivia could feel herself drawing close to him, despite herself, just to hear him. That was all. Nothing more. "Yet I wish to make a wreath well, and every Fitzroy says that you are the best."

Olivia glanced over at the trestle tables. For a moment, she thought her sisters and cousins had been standing there, watching her and Luke have this strange argument that wasn't an argument.

But as she looked over at them, every Fitzroy was suddenly very busy in whatever it was that they were doing. Perhaps too busy.

"Where is the gold thread?" asked Esther loudly.

"You're not having it until I am finished with it."

"Finished? You'll be all day at that speed."

"Fine," said Olivia warily. "I will show you. You can watch me start my wreath and then...then you can do your own. Are we agreed?"

Why was it that whenever Luke smiled, he seemed...predatory. Hungry. Olivia swallowed. The Luke she knew and loved, even if she had never admitted it to another soul, was kind, yes, but there was a mischief about him that had made her laugh until she cried when she was younger.

She wasn't laughing now.

"It's a bargain," said Luke, putting out his hand.

Olivia looked down at it. Shaking hands. It was not something young ladies did, not in polite society. Touching a gentleman?

But Luke wasn't just a gentleman, was he? In the eyes of her family, he was just one of them—almost an extension of the Fitzroy clan.

And to her...

Olivia reached out slowly and placed her hand in Luke's—and a rush of heat, desire she had never before known, poured through her. She wanted to leap into his arms, she wanted to crush her lips upon his. *She wanted...*

She wanted him. A want that seemed to glow between her legs, a want that could not be quenched by a mere handshake.

Olivia dropped his hand as swiftly as if she had been burned. Looking up at Luke, her eyes wide, she saw a strange expression fleetingly dance across his lips.

And then it was gone.

"So," he said quietly. "Where is your wire frame?"

"Wire frame," repeated Olivia, unsure how she was standing up. "Wire—for the wreath! Yes."

"Here's one," said Joy a little too conveniently, leaning over to pop one in Olivia's hands.

Olivia glared at her presumably eavesdropping cousin, who grinned.

"Always here to help."

Taking a deep breath and praying this whole escapade would be over before she truly embarrassed herself, Olivia moved to the trestle table. So. Greenery.

"You want to start with some larger bits of greenery, and then you can fill in the gaps with the holly and ivy," she said in a rush. "If Lucy leaves any for us."

"I've not taken too much!"

"And how do you weave it in?" Luke asked.

He was leaning close to her—to her wreath, Olivia told herself sternly. This was a family tradition, one she did every year. She just had to treat it like any other year.

As though a handsome gentleman she had been obsessed with for years wasn't inches from her.

"Just shove it in," said Olivia, praying none of her cousins paid too much attention to the way Luke was standing. Did he need to be so close? Surely he could see the way he was affecting her. Affecting her breathing.

"And then you carefully weave in the others," said Luke quietly, his breath once again on her neck.

Olivia fumbled with the ribbon. "Y-Yes. Yes, like this."

Focusing on the wreath would make it easier to ignore him, she was sure. Gazing hard at the ribbon, Olivia gently moved it in and out of the wire frame—and then she gasped. A pair of hands had joined hers, helping her to move the ribbon, Luke's searingly hot fingers brushing up against hers.

Olivia tried to stay calm. It was just a wreath!

"You do that so well."

"You are not so bad yourself," Olivia whispered.

The ribbon's movement slowed, but Luke's fingers had somehow managed to get entwined in hers.

"I don't want to force myself onto your company, you know," he said quietly. "I just…we were always good friends, you and I."

Olivia's heart sank, and she pulled her fingers away, brushing down her skirts as something to distract her.

Good friends. Well, she should have known that was what this was really about. Luke was lonely; his parents were gone, and he had no siblings to host him this Christmas. He had the Fitzroys, and they were the closest in age. They were friends.

And that was all. Any fanciful notions that she had managed to get into her head were just that, fanciful.

Olivia swallowed. "I…I am sorry for ignoring you. At dinner."

She could feel the smile on his face, feel the warmth in her body stir.

"Why did you?"

Olivia had barely heard him; Luke's murmur had been low, dark, full of an emotion she didn't understand. "I…I…"

"Come on Olivia, keep up!" beamed Harmony from the other side of the table. "Oh—Lord Kingsley. I hope I wasn't interrupting anything."

Olivia's stomach churned. Why did her cousins have to tease her so? Wasn't it obvious that not only was nothing happening, but that nothing ever would?

"No, nothing," she said as breezily as she could muster. "I think I will finish my wreath over here."

Without a second glance, Olivia lifted her wire frame and strode down the room, leaving a litter of unattached greenery in her path.

CHAPTER FOUR

NEVER BEFORE HAD Olivia quite examined the ceiling above her in such minute detail.

It was the same ceiling as ever. She had slept in this end of corridor bedchamber for her entire life—or at least, since she had left the nursery, which felt like a very long time ago at the moment.

There was a slight crack in one corner. Olivia had mapped that crack; sailed down it when she believed it to be a river, attacked it when she believed it a snake.

But now all she could see was the twirl of ribbon that had twisted between her hands, and the hands of Luke Kingsley. Hands which were strong, yet gentle. Hands that brushed up against hers surely by accident, Olivia told herself, and it was quite foolish to get so excited about it all.

"And then you carefully weave in the others."

"Y-Yes. Yes, like this."

Olivia swallowed. The sun had set hours ago, the candles been put out, yet still she lay here, unable to sleep, unable to become drowsy as her mind whirled through the events of the last few days.

Ever since Luke Kingsley had arrived at Chalcroft.

But it was all so foolish. Nothing had occurred! A few awkward moments, times when she had made a complete fool of herself, one or two misunderstandings, and an apology which she wished she had not made.

She had nothing to apologize for.

True, she had attempted to keep Luke—Lord Kingsley—at arm's length since he had arrived, but that was to be expected. She was a young lady, and he a gentleman. They were no longer children, could no longer ignore her sisters. They would attract attention—misinformed attention, maybe, but attention nonetheless—if she were to spend too much time with him.

Olivia tried her best to convince herself, but it was a rather poor argument.

She knew the truth. She knew it was only her desire for him, her affection for him which made her cheeks blush, which raised her heartrate, which made it impossible, it seemed, for her to be in the same room as him without making a complete ass of herself.

Even in the chill of her bedchamber, the fire long gone out, Olivia could feel the heat of shame pour through her as she remembered how close she had been to him at the wreath making trestle table.

So close, and yet not close enough. Not enough to fulfil the daydreams she had indulged in, when she and Luke were alone, and he came close to her as he had in the gun room, but this time with quite a different intent.

And it was all so foolish. Yes, Jemima, Caroline, and Harmony were married, but most of the Fitzroy cousins were either too young, or too intelligent to settle for anything less than perfection, Olivia told herself sternly. She was hardly on the shelf!

She might meet a number of people when she went into Town next year.

But lying to herself was simply not the answer. It did not work. She knew herself better than that. Twisting in her bed, she turned from facing the window to facing the wall.

It would not matter how many people she met, how many eligible gentlemen wandered into her path, how many introductions were made, how many times her parents whispered that so-and-so had an excellent estate, and that person's title was noble and worthy of attention.

If they were not Luke Kingsley, Olivia knew she could not marry them.

Wed a man who did not make every single part of her body tingle? Spend her life alongside a man who was half as kind, half as charming...

Sighing heavily, Olivia tried closing her eyes. She tried counting sheep, a trick Katarina had sworn by, though their mother had always laughed. She tried pushing the bedlinens back in case she was too hot, and then hastily pulled them back toward her as she shivered.

It was no use.

Olivia sat bolt upright. This was impossible. Through the gloom of her bedchamber, she could just make out the hands of the clock on the other side of the room. Almost one o'clock in the morning, and she had not slept a wink.

She would look awful tomorrow. Would Luke notice the bags under her eyes? Would he ask her why she had not slept, perhaps guess that she had a childish crush on him? Would he laugh, think her ridiculous for thinking of him like that?

Still sitting up, Olivia sighed heavily.

"If you are not going to go to sleep," came a muffled voice from the bed of Isabella pushed against the other side of the bedchamber, "go away."

Olivia scowled in the darkness. It really was most unfair that Isabella was forced to sleep in her bedchamber. While the house was large, it was not large enough to easily accommodate most of the Fitzroy family.

Isabella's bedchamber had been given over to Joy and Harmony, and a small bed placed in her elder sister's room. The bed had been pushed against the wall as though that would prevent Olivia from noticing her quiet solitude was being disturbed. Although admittedly, it was Isabella's quiet that was being disturbed at the moment.

"I am sorry," whispered Olivia wretchedly. "I cannot sleep."

"Evidently," muttered Isabella, turning around herself to look at her older sister. "But I do not believe you are getting much help from moving about so. Why do you not go downstairs, get a drink of something—a glass of wine, something to make you drowsy?"

It was not the worst idea Olivia had ever heard. Wine was something she and her sisters were encouraged to indulge in at mealtimes but no other time, yet she always felt very sleepy afterward.

"Good idea."

"Of course it is," came the sleepy response from Isabella. "I thought of it. Now go away."

Though it was rather irritating to be essentially turned out of one's own bedchamber, Olivia had to admit it was better than lying there, not sleeping. Slipping on her nightrobe over her nightgown and fumbling as she put on her slippers, Olivia did not bother lighting a candle to descend.

What was the point? She knew Chalcroft perfectly, every inch of it. The day she needed a candle to navigate its corridors was the day she should be leaving it.

Her bedchamber door only creaked a little as she closed it. The corridor was silent, dark, empty. Everyone else was asleep, enjoying their slumber. It was difficult not to be a little envious.

Treading softly, Olivia crept down the corridor and reached the top of the staircase. She could not help but be reminded of the moment when Luke had taken her hand only yesterday.

The touch of his hand on her arm. The strength, his strength holding her as she had almost tripped on the stair. The comforting warmth of him, as though he was always supposed to be there, by her side, her true support.

Olivia swallowed, her hand resting on the top of the banister as she stood in thought.

Was it merely hours ago? So much had happened since then,

or at least, Olivia reminded herself, nothing had. And nothing would.

Luke Kingsley simply did not see her that way. If he did, would not something have happened in that time? Would he not have said something, would not the passion she felt for him have been reflected in his eyes?

And you never know, Olivia wondered as she stepped down the staircase, the darkness seeming to muffle her steps. She may just meet a gentleman from the gaggle her father invited, and discover her feelings for Luke Kingsley were nothing more than a passing fancy.

Olivia had to smile wryly as she reached the bottom of the staircase. Not that that was very likely.

The drawing room was on the other side of the house from here, and really Olivia would have reached it quicker if she had taken the servants' staircase instead of the main one.

But that would have prevented her from enjoying the journey through Chalcroft on her own. It was strange; even when one lived in one's house all year round, it was rare to see it alone, at its best. When decorated for Christmas.

There were springs of holly and ivy over all the paintings in the great hall and in the corridor that led to the kitchens. Elegant gold bells fashioned out of paper and painted had been placed over doorframes throughout the house. Leonora had been most determined when she had first come here, Olivia had always been told, that the servants' quarters should be just as decorated as the main house. Why should the servants not have a little Christmas cheer?

None of the candles in the wall brackets were lit, but Olivia continued on her way, and soon she reached the drawing room door.

But she hesitated. Were her eyes deceiving her, or was that…

Light. Light, slowly spilling out from around the large oak door. Light? Down here, at this hour?

Olivia bit her lip. If one of her uncles was still awake, reading a book or enjoying a glass of his favorite liquor, he may not appreciate the interruption—but surely it was too late at night, or early in the morning, for something like that?

Reaching out gingerly, Olivia grasped the latch and hesitated once more. She had no wish to speak to anyone else; she wished for a glass of wine and then bed.

But she was a Fitzroy. There wouldn't be anyone in this drawing room that she did not want to see.

A comforting smile on her face, Olivia turned the handle, opened the door, and stepped into the room.

"I hope you do not mind the intrusion," she said brightly as she turned to face the person she was now sharing the drawing room with. "But I…"

Olivia's voice trailed away as her breath caught in her lungs.

In a house full of Fitzroys, she had managed to walk into a room at the dead of night which contained Luke Kingsley.

He was seated by the dying glow of the fire, a glass of whiskey in his hand, his eyes were wide as he beheld her.

And no wonder. Olivia pulled her nightrobe around her as tightly as possible and wished to goodness she had never conceived of such a foolish idea as this. Worse, it had not even been her own idea, but Isabella's. She should not have listened to her!

A glass of wine? She should merely have suffered in silence, allowing Isabella to sleep. Because now…

Olivia was only a few yards from Luke, who was fully dressed, though his cravat was undone at the neck. She attempted not to look at his throat, wiry dark hair protruding and promising alluring delights, which she certainly should not be thinking about…

Her mouth was dry, heart beating painfully against a chest that seemed to be rising and falling with hurried breaths.

She needed to say something. Why did he not say something?

For some reason, Luke appeared to be just as astonished to see her as she did him.

Only then did Olivia realize that though he was fully dressed, she...she was in her nightgown and robe. She was practically undressed!

"Olivia," said Luke, hastily rising to his feet.

"Oh, you don't need to—"

"What are you doing down here at this hour?" he asked in a low voice.

Olivia swallowed. She could not remember the last time she and Luke had been alone—really alone, not like when they had been at the top of the staircase yesterday.

Years, perhaps. Maybe when they had decided to run away together, and had dressed up in his clothing. Or the time they had gone into the village to buy honey with stolen pennies, the sticky sweetness too tempting in the kitchen, and had been caught by Cook who was replenishing his own supplies.

Yet the Luke which stood before her was not the gangling youth she had adored and idolized. No, Luke was no child. He was a man. Though she was tall, he stood a few inches taller, and it was only now that Olivia noticed they were but a few feet from each other.

How had that happened? She had not moved, had she?

"Well, whatever reason it is, I must say that...that you look well."

Olivia flushed at the compliment. Was it a compliment? Surely not, if Luke had said it. They were childhood friends, after all. It was not his fault she had this strange affection for him.

"Do not be ridiculous," she said, dropping her gaze to her nightgown to halt the strange connection their gazes were making. "You cannot possibly mean that."

"Why not?"

Olivia looked up. Luke stood there, staring at her as though he had been waiting for her all along.

"You do not ask me what I am doing here," he said quietly, taking a step toward her.

Unconsciously, Olivia took a step back. "Well, it would be

unseemly to inquire as to a gentleman's private business."

"Private business?" Luke chuckled as he took another step toward her, and Olivia's legs hit the wall. She could retreat no further. "Dear Lord, Olivia, we have known each other for too long, surely, to hide our meaning."

Hide…hide our meaning? Olivia's eyes searched his own, but could not comprehend what he was speaking of. Meaning?

"We have known each other a long time," Olivia said quietly.

He was but a foot from her now, and Luke halted, examining her closely, as though expecting to find an answer to his questions.

Olivia barely knew how she would manage to speak, even if she had something to say. Her breath was caught in her lungs at the sheer proximity to the man. His broad shoulders and height blocked out the rest of the drawing room, so that all she could see was him. Luke.

And what a sight it was.

If she had been bolder, like Jemima perhaps, or Katarina, she would have leaned forward and kissed the man who seemed designed to taunt her and tease her about what she could not have.

If only Luke had never come to Chalcroft for Christmas.

"Just because I have known you for a long time," said Luke in a low voice, his eyes never leaving hers, "that does not mean I do not know a beautiful woman when I see one."

It took a moment for the words to register, but when Olivia's mind finally caught up, her jaw dropped. "You—you cannot mean that!"

"Why not?" said Luke urgently. "You think I stayed down here for my own amusement, staring into the fire alone?"

Olivia's heart was pattering so furiously, she thought it would burst, but it was nothing to the strange heat that was pooling between her legs.

Did he…did he mean what she thought, what she hoped?

"I haven't been able to stop thinking about you, you and your stupid wreath all day!" Luke let out with a dry laugh. "Dear God, Olivia, it's like you're designed to tease me. Perfection, just out of reach."

Olivia licked her lips and he groaned, placing a palm on the wall beside her as he hung his head.

"You don't even know what you do to me," he said quietly. "You have no idea."

"I have every idea."

Olivia did not know what made her say it. Perhaps it was the way he leaned toward her, his heady scent tantalizingly just out of reach. Perhaps it was the very real pain he uttered as he spoke.

But she knew this was the moment. If she was ever to be honest, to share what she really felt, it was now.

Wasn't it?

Luke looked up, his eyes focused on her mouth. "What did you say?"

Olivia hesitated, but finally managed to speak. "I have…I have every idea. You…I…you do not know what you do to me, Luke."

Without taking his eyes from her, Luke placed his other palm on the wall, entrapping her now within his arms, but he made no move to approach her. Olivia ached at the distance of a few inches, but she could not close them.

"Tell me."

Olivia looked up into his fierce eyes. "What?"

All she had been able to manage was a whisper, but he heard her. "Tell me. Tell me what I do to you."

Heat seared her cheeks. Tell—tell Luke what he made her feel! It was scandalous, it was ridiculous—Olivia was not entirely sure she even had the words to do so!

Luke did not move his hands, but he did close the gap between them, and Olivia gasped, gasped at the intensity of the feeling of Luke's chest pressed up against hers.

It was too much, too much to bear, and the words came spilling out before she could do anything to stop them.

"You make me warm, Luke." Olivia looked up into his eyes, for the first time full of desire for her, and though she could not understand why someone like him would ever look at her, knowing she would make a fool of herself if she continued, the words kept coming. "Hot. I want you to touch me, touch me with your fingers, and kiss me, and show me you want me as…as I want you."

The words seemed to hang in the air, condemning her as a strumpet, but Olivia did not look away from the gentleman who had been her companion as a child and now appeared so aloof, so distant—

Luke's lips crushed against hers, and Olivia moaned at the intensity of the pleasure he gave her. He possessed her, teasing her lips with his own as she sank into his arms, the wall and his strength just about holding her upright.

For her legs could not hold her, not as this scalding heat rushed through her body as Luke's lips teased hers open. Unsure what she was doing but knowing it was giving her more pleasure than Olivia ever thought possible, she allowed him entrance, welcomed him in—and was rewarded with the tingle of unknown and untasted sweetness as his tongue ravished her own.

"Luke," she whispered as they drew breath, but she was unable to say more as Luke's hands moved from the wall to her waist, pulling her closer.

Olivia's hands moved to his neck, her fingers entwining themselves in his hair, pulling him closer, because there was no such thing as close enough.

She wanted him, wanted him as a woman wanted a man, and Olivia knew she should stop, knew this was reckless, knew that no words of affection had been shared between them, only lust— but in this moment, lust was enough.

"Olivia, dear God," murmured Luke as he pulled away but kept his hands on her waist. "You…you have no idea how long I have wanted to do that."

Olivia stared, hardly able to believe what she was seeing,

what she was hearing. Luke, in her arms, wanting her, wanting her as she wanted him.

"I do not think you know how long I have wanted you to do that," she admitted shyly, and Luke chuckled.

"Well, if I had known that, I would have sent your sisters and cousins away and taken you right there on the wreath trestle tables."

Lying back on that table, her skirts pushed up to her waist, Luke above her, about to—

"Olivia," Luke whispered, lowering his head and stealing another kiss—though was it a theft if Olivia gave it to him willingly?

She clung to him, desperate for this moment never to end, but knowing that it would, knowing this could lead nowhere. For what had Luke said of affection, of devotion, of commitment?

Nothing. He no longer saw her as a child any more, that was for certain, but he did not see her as a prospective bride, that was equally true. He desired her, that was all. In this moment, that was enough.

For in this moment, she needed no promises. She had him in her arms, his lips on hers, his fingers tight around her waist, and that was all she could manage at present.

The thought of more…

"No."

As though he had read her mind, Luke dropped her as though she had scalded him, and took a staggering step backward.

"Luke?" Olivia said quietly. She had offended him, she knew that, even if she did not know how.

Luke shook his head. "Christ, I could almost…but I mustn't. I am here on your father's invitation, Olivia, and I must not…even if you are…"

Olivia smiled. He desired her. A rush of delicious power enveloped her heart. She had never known the power of having a gentleman want her, and it was rather intoxicating.

"You did nothing wrong," she said quietly. "Nothing…nothing I did not want."

His eyes met hers, and Olivia almost melted where she stood. And yet, it was not enough. She wanted more—more that she knew Luke could not give her.

"It…it is time we went to bed," Luke said heavily, "and in different bedchambers," he added with a mischievous smile. "No matter how much I may wish the opposite. There, I have offended you."

Olivia raised a hand to her cheeks. They were certainly warm, but due to no offence, but rather desire. Her and Luke in the same bedchamber…

"You have not offended," she said shyly. "I just…I want—"

Luke groaned. "Definitely time for me to step away from you, you siren. If I am to have any self-control and dance with you at the Christmas Eve ball, you must let me walk away."

Olivia took a step forward, almost without thinking, and Luke laughed as he took a corresponding step away from her and toward the door to the hall.

"You minx," he said ruefully. "I wish you had come down sooner, but as it is…good night, Olivia."

He was gone before she could say another word.

Olivia stared around the empty room. She could still taste Luke Kingsley on her lips. Nothing in the drawing room had changed. She was not entirely sure what she had expected, but somehow, she felt as though the world should be different.

She certainly was. What was she supposed to make of all that?

CHAPTER FIVE

"THERE YOU ARE! I thought you would never get up—she was so drowsy this morning."

Olivia smiled weakly as Isabella heralded her arrival to the breakfast room the following morning.

"Drowsy?" repeated Jemima, a frown on her face displaying her immediate concern. "Why?"

That was the trouble with a large and raucous family, Olivia thought to herself as she sank quietly into a seat just vacated by Katarina, rushing off somewhere for goodness knows what.

One could not even oversleep by—Olivia glanced at the grandfather clock in the corner of the room. Two hours. That was rather surprising.

Still. She did not deserve to have absolutely everyone in the place comment on her lateness, even if most of the Fitzroys had broken their fasts already.

There were still a number of people at the breakfast table. Esther and Lucy were gossiping over a letter they had received from their sister, who Olivia had heard was visiting her future husband's parents for Christmas—a real shame, for she greatly liked her cousin Arabella—and Maria was silently finishing up a cup of tea, clearly in the hope that no one would talk to her.

Their mother Leonora was at one end of the table hidden behind a newspaper, which was unlike her, and her Uncle Arthur was reading a letter with a concerned look on his face. Olivia had to assume it was from one of his daughters, three of whom were not at Chalcroft. Who else could be sending him post here?

The breakfast room was filled with weak wintery sunlight, bright, but with no warmth. The large bay windows that overlooked the lawn faced the south and so welcomed in as much light as it could, even in these dark months.

Not that it was making much of a difference today. In the midwinter of England, one was fortunate to have any sunlight at all, and Olivia could not help but smile at the attempt the day was making to be bright.

It didn't matter if the day was cold, at least in her opinion. She would rather have bright and crisp, then warm and dull. Besides, there was enough fire rushing through her veins to keep her warm.

"You do look a little tired."

Olivia started as she reached out for some toast. Her mother was looking at her appraisingly, newspaper lowered, as though she was attempting to decide what remedy to give her.

Her mother's remedies. Leonora had always said her knowledge of plants and herbs came from her grandmother's side, that all Italians knew it.

Her daughters were not so sure. Nettle tea was all very well, but after four cups, one would rather take the stuffed nose than another sip.

"I am quite well, I assure you," said Olivia hastily, foreseeing some sort of cold dandelion compress in her future. "Just a little tired, that is all."

Most of the table returned to their conversations, or in Maria's case, her determination not to be noticed by anyone.

Olivia took the opportunity to pour herself a cup of tea. That was what she needed, tea. Everything could be solved once she had a cup of—

"Kingsley!"

Startled, Olivia's fingers slipped. Hot scalding tea poured

across the white linen tablecloth, staining it a muddy brown.

"Olivia, *fate attenzione*|!" her mother exclaimed, slipping into her Italian as she so often did when irritated. *"Please be careful, that is my best linen!"*

"Watch out!" Esther lifted up Arabella's letter hastily to prevent it from becoming stained, and Lucy giggled as Joy came into the room, saw the disaster, and immediately walked out.

Olivia could barely take in all the ruckus at the table as people attempted to stave off the impending wash of tea. She was too busy looking up at the gentleman who had just entered the room.

Luke Kingsley.

"You minx. I wish you had come down sooner, but as it is…good night, Olivia."

Olivia hoped to goodness her family assumed it was due to her clumsiness with the teapot, and not anything to do with the entrance of the Lord Kingsley.

He looked remarkable. Hair still a little tousled, as though his valet did absolutely nothing to keep it tidy, and his cravat once more tied in an elaborate knot, which Olivia could not understand how anyone could untie.

Images flashed through her mind of Luke pressing her up against the wall, of him kissing her, of her fingers reaching forward and hastily pulling at the knot, forcing it to undo and fall to the floor, as the rest of their clothes joined it…

Olivia hastily put the teapot down. She was not to be trusted with such a thing, if such vulgar images were going to rush through her mind!

It had taken her another hour to fall asleep last night when she had finally reached her bedchamber. Isabella had been asleep, naturally, and she had attempted not to disturb her, but the memories of her encounter with Luke were more than enough to disturb her.

What had he been playing at? What did he mean when he said he wished she had come down sooner?

That he desired her, she could no longer refute; but he had

said nothing of her character, of his affections for her. Although she had to admit, there had not been much talking from either side. She had not exactly admitted her affections for him, either.

Olivia had worried then, in the early hours of the morning, what she would do or say when she saw him. Should she pretend it had never happened? Would he himself regret it—had Luke been too deep in his cups to really know what he had been about?

The thought made her nauseous. That such a thing could happen and be so special to her and yet nothing to him...

It would not be borne.

And so Olivia had concocted no clever plan or scheme to keep herself calm when she saw him—though admittedly, she would have preferred it if she had not made such a scene by spilling tea absolutely everywhere.

"A new pot, I think," said Leonora amid the mingled exclaims and laughter.

A footman immediately bowed his head and retreated, presumably to fetch one.

Olivia could still feel heat on her cheeks. "I do apologize, Mama."

Her mother nodded curtly. That was one of the wonderful things about her parents, Olivia had always thought. They would accept no pretense as to blame, but if one admitted fault and apologized, the thing was forgotten.

"No harm, I suppose," she said. "You are tired, aren't you?"

"Tired?" said Luke brightly as he moved around the table. "I am, rather."

All eyes moved to him—all eyes save Olivia's. She was highly conscious for the first time that there were only two empty seats at the table; one between her mother and Esther, and one...one beside her.

Surely he would not be so bold as to sit beside her? Would he?

No, Olivia said to calm herself. He would not be so much of a fool to—

"Good morning, Olivia," Luke said brightly as he sat before her and placed a non-tea-soaked napkin on his lap. "It appears we both slept ill."

Olivia could hardly look into his face. How could he say such a thing? Did he wish for the entire family to guess what they…what they had…

"Such a shame," said Lucy with a shake of her head. "I thought Katarina looked tired too—a little preoccupied, perhaps."

"Too much excitement about the Christmas Eve ball," said Jemima matter-of-factly, as though she could diagnose tiredness in her sleep. "That'll be it, mark me. When the ball is over, everyone will sleep like logs."

"How many people are coming to the ball, Aunt Leonora?" asked Lucy.

The conversation about the ball continued, and Olivia was relieved to see she was not required to contribute. Murmurs of candle orders and gentlemen callers, of Katarina's outburst the other day, and whether or not the musicians would get here through the snow…

"So," said Luke in a low murmur as he reached across Olivia for the marmalade. "You did not sleep well."

Olivia shot a glance at him and saw a mischievous smile dance about his lips. How could he speak so…so calmly? Was his heart not racing inside him? Did he not find the very sight of her enough to make his stomach lurch?

And if not…Olivia felt her cheeks flush. If not, then why on earth had he kissed her? Why had he said those things, made her feel, made her say…those things?

The memory of the words he had managed to exact out of her seared through Olivia's mind, as if permanently branded there.

"You make me warm, Luke. Hot. I want you to touch me, touch me with your fingers, and kiss me, and show me you want me as…as I want you."

It was enough to make her want to melt into the carpet and

never face him again—yet Luke was carefully buttering his toast and opening up the jar of marmalade as though nothing had even happened between them. As though this was a normal breakfast, with normal conversation, and nothing untoward or wonderful had occurred.

Olivia swallowed. As though this happened all the time. As though it was one of many kisses he had stolen from ladies against drawing room walls.

Was that possible?

That was the trouble with a childhood friend growing up, she thought fiercely as she pulled jam toward her and started liberally spreading it across her own toast, as though that could distract her from her own thoughts.

He had been charming and wonderful and handsome, and now…

Now she was not sure whether she knew Luke at all. Lord Luke Kingsley seemed to be a world away from the boy she had played with and adored.

"Sleep eluded you, it appears much as she eluded me," he continued with a wicked grin. "Such a shame."

Olivia glared. Well, he was asking for nothing less. How could he speak to her like that, as though they were mere indifferent acquaintances?

"I slept very well, thank you," she said stiffly. "When I returned to my—I slept very well."

Olivia took a large bite of her toast and chewed her mouthful while looking around the breakfast room, hoping to join the conversation of another. Surely someone would say something of interest that could distract her for a moment.

Anything, rather than talk to Luke.

"Where is Katarina?" her mother was saying. "I have not seen her since—"

"She was arguing with Uncle William the last I saw her," said Jemima. Olivia had to smile slightly at that; Jemima never did know when to hold her tongue. "Something about the stables, though I heard no more."

A concerned look was spreading across Leonora's face. "The stables? What was she doing—there you are!"

Katarina had stormed into the breakfast room, a terrible temper on her face.

Olivia swallowed her mouthful and glanced quickly at her mother. Yes, there was the same temper rising.

"How dare you tell me where I can and cannot go in my own home!" Katarina exploded, stopping just before her mother and clearly unconcerned with making a scene before sisters, cousins, and guest. "I am more than old enough to—"

"This is not a question of age, nor maturity, one of which you are painfully lacking," snapped back her mother, equally unashamed to be rowing in public. "This is about propriety, and your complete lack of it!"

Olivia dropped her head and took a sip of the small amount of tea that managed to remain in her cup. Well, it would not be a Christmas, would it, if Katarina and their mother were not bickering?

"Olivia," murmured Luke under the ruckus, "I have not told anyone. You know that, don't you?"

How could he speak of it here—with her family merely seats away?

But as she glanced up, she could see that Maria and their cousins were absorbed in the argument that Katarina appeared determined to have with Leonora, though Olivia could not entirely make out what all the fuss was about. Kitty wanted to go somewhere that her mother did not approve of? Why?

Instead, she looked back at Luke, and her stomach lurched painfully. He was so handsome; that charming smile looking a little too knowing, it was true, but he was also too close.

Far too close. Olivia shivered, unable to stop herself at the memory of those fingers, so close to her, which had merely hours before been holding her waist. Holding her close. Closer than she had ever believed possible for a gentleman and a lady to be…

"You...you will not tell a soul?" Olivia found herself asking quietly.

She had done her best to keep the desperation out of her voice, but it appeared by the look on his face—a little hurt—that she had not succeeded.

"You think I would?" Luke said quietly. "You think I would betray your trust? That I would...would crow about such a thing?"

Olivia looked down, unable to hold his gaze. She had not thought that precisely—and she was not entirely sure who she was worried he would tell.

There were no other gentlemen here, save for her father and his two brothers. Except for the gentlemen coming for the Christmas Eve ball...but Luke did not know them. He was not the sort of gentleman to boast of such things to people he did not even know...was he?

The Luke she had known as a child would certainly not have done such things. But this Luke had gone to Oxford, gone on a Grand Tour. Had spent a Season in London.

He was Lord Kingsley now, not her Luke. How well did she truly know him after all these years?

"I am not pretending to fully understand what happened last night," Luke said quietly. He had placed his toast back onto his plate. His hand was resting beside hers on the table. So close. "Desire is a strange thing, Olivia, you must know that. It does not always reveal its next move. Its next decision."

Heat was flowing through Olivia's veins at the mention of 'desire'. Did he know how she felt about him?

"You make me warm, Luke. Hot. I want you to touch me, touch me with your fingers, and kiss me, and show me you want me as...as I want you."

True, she had revealed the physical impact he was having on her—but she had said nothing of her feelings, her devotion to him.

Could he guess?

Olivia looked over, her eyes meeting his, and a gasp escaped her throat. Luke was looking at her like...like the world had ended. Like they were the only two people in the world, let alone the room.

As though if he could just keep looking at her, then he would find solace in her eyes and nothing else.

"Desire," Luke said softly, taking her hand in his, "is untamed. Uncontrolled. It is for us to manage, but that does not mean we know where it is going. We merely follow and discover."

"Like...like last night," Olivia managed to whisper.

His hand was warm. Strong. Comforting. It was also reminding her all too well just what it was like to have Luke's hands on her waist. Pulling her closer. As though nothing was close enough. As if he wished to be closer to her still.

There was a vague sense at the back of Olivia's mind that they were in the breakfast room with her family and what they were doing was most unseemly—but it did not seem to matter. They faded from view.

There was only Luke.

There was a devilish smile on his face as he gently stroked her hand. "Like last night. Last night I saw you, and I wanted you, Olivia."

"Wanted...wanted to kiss me?"

"Oh, far more than that," murmured Luke as he refused to look away from her. "Wanted things a young lady like you, brought up well, a good family, a good name, could not even comprehend."

Olivia shivered. She did. She knew, in theory at least, what a gentleman and a lady could explore together. How they could share pleasure. How they could touch and kiss and give themselves to each other.

They had been speaking in such low voices that it was only now that Olivia noticed that she and Luke had twisted in their seats to face each other. Her head was low, and so was his, their foreheads almost touching. Their lips merely inches apart.

"I...I know," she found herself saying, the moment between them lengthening, causing ripples of anticipation to seep through her body. An ache was building, an ache she did not recognize but had felt before. Last night in the drawing room? "At least—I think I know."

A low groan escaped Luke's throat. "Dear God, Olivia, don't—don't say such things to me. There is so much you do not understand."

Olivia twisted her hand in his and intertwined her fingers with his. "Then show me."

"Olivia! I said pass the jam!"

Olivia and Luke sprang apart, hands returning to their sides as she passed Jemima the jam.

She had been absolutely certain her cousin would remark not only on the delayed response to her request, but also on her scalding red cheeks, on the way she had been so closely seated with Luke.

Jemima said nothing but continued speaking with her aunt. Olivia blinked. Katarina had gone; she had not noticed her departure.

"That is the trouble with these young girls," Jemima was saying defiantly, as though she had raised several dozen. "They did not know when it is time to let go and obey their—"

"Like you do, you mean?" asked Lucy, her color heightened. "Like you listen to our father?"

"I did not mean—"

"So, Olivia," said Luke bracingly in a loud, clear voice, as though nothing at all had occurred between them. "What is your plan for this sunny morning?"

Olivia stared at him, utterly bewildered. How did he do it? One moment he was speaking of desire, of passion, of the ways that a gentleman and a lady...

And the next, he was speaking of the weather.

A tendril of doubt curled around her heart. Was this a game

to him? Was this just something he did for fun, a way to entertain himself while he was staying with friends?

With a sinking heart, Olivia had to own, even to herself, that it was possible. She had never seen Luke in the company of others, beyond her own family. It was impossible to know precisely what he did when not at Chalcroft.

"I...I do not know," was all she managed.

"Well, whatever you decide, I would greatly like to accompany you," Luke said with a bold smile before taking a sip of tea.

Olivia smiled weakly. She would just have to hope that no one else heard that. "I am sure you have many other things to be doing, Lord Kingsley."

Luke raised an eyebrow. "Lord Kingsley, am I?"

"You are indeed," said Olivia, rising from the table and swallowing. She had to say it, she had to protect herself. "And I think that is perhaps what you shall stay."

CHAPTER SIX

"I THEREFORE CONSIDER this Christmas Eve ball open!"

There were cheers as Olivia's father threw open the front doors to Chalcroft and welcomed in the waiting guests.

It was always the way with him, Olivia thought with a wry smile as she stood in the great hall with her sisters and cousins. Her father simply could not help but lean into the theatrics of anything he put his mind to—and though the Fitzroys rarely hosted balls, only two of their daughters *out*, there was always far more than a song and dance to an occasion when her father was permitted to preside over things.

"Come on through, come on through," he was saying to some of their neighbors. Olivia recognized most of them from church, though they looked a little strange at present, all wrapped in their furs against the freezing cold. "We have music and dancing in the ballroom, food put out in the dining room—yes, of course, there is roast lamb…"

"So many gentlemen," murmured Joy.

Olivia turned to her, and to her great surprise, her cousin flushed at being overheard. Joy, embarrassed? She was always jesting, always ensuring laughter.

"Indeed," Olivia said. "There are a great number of acquaintances of ours who did not go to London for the Season this year."

Olivia glanced at the guests pouring in. The Marnmouths, the de Petras, half the Axwick family…

"You should have plenty of partners for the dancing," she continued in a low tone, seeing whether she could get Joy to smile again.

But her flush deepened, and Joy scowled. "I did not ask—I am not desperate for partners, Olivia, and I hope you will not say that I am so! I merely remarked on the number of gentlemen!"

She stalked away across the dining room, where Maria was ready to gravitate.

Olivia stared. It was such a strange response from Joy that she was quite unable to account for it. True, her sister Harmony had been married now for over a year; how strange to have one's younger sister married before you.

Perhaps that was it. Perhaps Joy was feeling the pressure from her parents to find a match.

Gratitude to her parents for not pushing such expectations on her seared Olivia's heart. There her father was, helping the Countess of Marnmouth off with her pelisse and shaking the snow off on the floor so as not to offend either his wife or the butler.

Her mother was about here somewhere—ah yes. Olivia could hear her voice in the ballroom, instructing the musicians, God help them. She should probably go through and protect them.

Olivia sighed. That was the trouble with being the eldest of four sisters; there was always some sort of responsibility.

"Please, come on into the ballroom," she said in a slightly raised voice, indicating the way with her hands.

Esther and Lucy, dressed in matching gowns, giggled and rushed off in the direction of the ballroom, while a few of the guests bowed their heads in acknowledgement and started following her cousins.

Katarina was leaning against the wall near the door to the ballroom. Olivia slowed when she reached her.

"You know, I do not think I have seen you these last three

days together," she remarked. "Not really. Where on earth have you been, Kitty?"

A dark scowl covered her sister's face. "Mind your own business."

It was enough to make Olivia halt altogether. The rudeness was almost expected with Kitty, but the anger, the rage? "I beg your pardon?"

"I said mind your own business, and leave your nose out of mine," muttered Katarina, her eyes low.

Olivia stared. Katarina was not always the most genial of her sisters—that was surely Isabella—but she could not recall such rudeness from any Fitzroy in…well, years. Even Maria, the baby of the family, had not given into her temper like this in months. Well, weeks. At least an entire week.

She examined her sister. Katarina looked…different. Olivia could not precisely put her finger on what had changed, but something certainly had. There was a…a brightness around the eyes that had not been there before. Though Katarina had not yet danced—the musicians were still receiving instructions from their mother, from what Olivia could hear—Kitty looked a little flushed.

What on earth had happened?

Had she become so absorbed with Luke and whatever was— or was not—happening between them that she had missed something crucial with her sister?

"Kitty," said Olivia, dropping her voice so that they would not be overheard by the guests now passing by to enter the ballroom. "You…you do know that you can come to me with anything?"

"This is…this isn't…'tis nothing to do with you."

Why would her sister not look at her? It was most odd, and if there wasn't a ball happening right in that moment, Olivia would have taken her sister aside to a quiet spot—the library, perhaps— and made sure to get the secret out of her.

After all, how disastrous or exciting could it be, truly? They saw no one, had no guests but Luke…

Olivia's heart turned cold. She looked again at her sister, and saw the signs which she had noticed in herself. The inability to look at one's sisters, flushed cheeks, utterly helpless to talk about what was going on in her head…

Surely not. Surely Luke would not be so callous, so destructive as to make love to her sister Katarina? Was it possible that she was not the only Fitzroy that Luke had been kissing, had been whispering sweet nothings to? Was it all a lie? A joke? A trick?

Olivia's breath was short as she attempted to think. She needed to find out—but how to ask such a delicate question?

"Katarina Fitzroy," Olivia said in almost a whisper. "You haven't…you would not…there have been no interactions with a g-gentleman that you want to tell me about, are there?"

Katarina's face lost all its color in an instant. "Who—who told you?"

It was Olivia's worst fears revealed, but worst of all, she was unable to continue speaking with her sister in private.

"What are you two doing here, standing at the sidelines?" Lucy said with a broad grin, placing loving hands on both her and Katarina's shoulders. "This is your house, your Christmas Eve ball! The dancing is about to begin! Come on!"

There was nothing for it. A million questions rushing through her mind, every single one of them causing pain to ricochet through her heart, Olivia had no choice but to smile blandly and follow her cousin into the ballroom.

The servants had outdone themselves with the decorations. There were more candles than Olivia had ever seen in one place, ribbons and bells, holly and ivy, even something that looked remarkably like gold fairy dust that had been gently brushed across the tables at one end where the punch bowl and glasses stood.

Yet Olivia could not enjoy the spectacle that made the Fitzroys' guests exclaim with delight. Not really.

Not now that she knew.

She was not special. She was not even unique. Luke had probably given Katarina the same old guff he had trotted out for her, and it appeared that both sisters were easily charmed by the gentleman's words.

And his kisses.

Olivia's stomach turned at the mere thought that Luke had taken not only her first kiss, but her sister's. It was barbaric! It was disgraceful! He should be called out!

Oh, if only she had a brother—or a male cousin. Someone other than her father who could call Luke out, then throw him out.

But as it was…

Olivia's keen eyes glanced around the room. He was not here. Well, perhaps that was all to the good.

"Dear me, you look quite done for, and the dancing hasn't even begun yet!"

Olivia turned to see Esther approaching her, a smile on her face. Olivia smiled weakly back. "Oh, I was just…just thinking."

Esther raised an eyebrow. She had pearls dotted about her hair that gleamed in the candlelight, and her delicate white gown looked beautiful against her red curls.

"Well, I hereby suggest that thinking is set aside, for now," she said good-naturedly. "There is far too much merriment to be had here, if you ask me."

Olivia's weak smile did not broaden. Yes, dancing. Merriment.

She had been so looking forward to it, too. If she was honest with herself, and that was the only person she would be truthful with, she could not bear the shame of revealing it to another…she had hoped that this would be a chance for Luke to declare himself. To ask her to dance, to make it clear to her family that she was the one he wanted.

The thought tasted bitter now. Her trust in him could never be restored.

"Goodness, I do not believe I have seen so many people at a

ball—a private one that is—since my father hosted one for Caroline and Stuart's engagement," Esther said cheerfully, as more guests poured into the ballroom. "There are nine of us Fitzroys, and last time there were ten lords in the line when you'll never guess—Stuart's uncle…"

Olivia nodded blandly as Esther told a story that was not very interesting. Yes, nine ladies dancing; but she had been certain that Luke would be here, to ascertain whether he could have her hand for the first dance. To ask for it. To plead with her, with that teasing smile on his lips.

And yet, he had still not appeared. Where was he? What was going on?

"—Olivia? Olivia, you haven't been listening to a word I have been saying, have you?"

"What?" said Olivia, blinking.

Esther came back into focus, and most unusually, she was scowling. "What has got into you today? You're as bad as Katarina!"

She wandered away to talk with Isabella and Maria, leaving Olivia feeling a little disgruntled.

Well, it was not as though it was her fault that Luke had raised all sorts of hopes within her, hopes that she did not truly understand, then dashed them to pieces before her eyes!

But no, it was worse than that. He had not done that precisely, had he? It had been Katarina who had ended all her hopes of something true and meaningful with Luke, and her sister had not even known it. That was the true tragedy of the thing. Luke had used them, used them both, and driven a wedge between them.

Olivia swallowed. She needed to find him. Find him and tell him precisely what she thought of him—he had to be made to see just how outrageous his behaviors—

"There you are!" Her mother looked a little flushed as she always did when she was making demands of other people in a language other than her native tongue. "You would think, wouldn't you, that musicians would know the best music to dance to, but they did not even plan on playing—"

"I am sure it will be wonderful, Mama," interrupted Olivia. "You have spoken with them now, after all."

Leonora sniffed. "Yes. Yes, I have. Well, I should go and find your father—the dancing is about to begin!"

Olivia watched her mother push her way through the crowd. There was something about being half Fitzroy, half Italian, she thought. She had inherited all the dramatic passion of the Italian side of her, and all the determination of the Fitzroys.

She would speak with him. Luke. She would find him, and tell him just how wrong he was to say such things to her, to…to touch her in that way.

What on earth could he have been saying to Kitty to make her pale like that?

Olivia swallowed. Now all she had to do was find him.

It was starting to feel a little like a crush in the ballroom—her father had evidently done what he always did, and invited too many people in the assumption that several of them would be unable to attend.

It appeared, however, that an invitation to a Fitzroy ball was too enticing to miss. As Olivia moved slowly through the crowd, hoping and yet desperately not hoping to come across Lord Luke Kingsley, snippets of conversations seemed to suggest that there had even been a few people who had left London to be able to attend tonight.

"A short journey really, and when one has an invitation from William Fitzroy—"

"—just as I had always thought it would look, and of course receiving an invitation to Chalcroft is such an honor…"

Olivia could not help but smile. It was pleasant, even in the midst of her suffering, to see just how respected the Fitzroy name was.

Not that Luke had any such respect. Olivia's stomach swooped as she caught sight of him.

He was standing by the punch table, a glass in his hand, and in his other hand…

Olivia froze. Though she was several yards away still, she could not move a single muscle.

Luke was standing there, holding the hand of her sister, Katarina. He was speaking to her in a low urgent voice, and Kitty's cheeks were pink.

Time seemed to stand still. Blood rushed through her ears, pounding so loudly, Olivia could no longer hear the conversations going on around her. She could not move, could not breathe.

Luke was holding Katarina's hand. Here. At the Fitzroy Christmas Eve ball, her Christmas Eve ball. When she had thought…had hoped…

A gentleman Olivia did not recognize stepped toward Katarina, asked her something, and was rudely dismissed by something Luke said.

It was true then. Olivia would not have believed it unless she had seen it with her very own eyes, but there it was. Luke would be dancing with Katarina, for what else could the young man have asked? And to be so instantly dismissed, for Katarina to not even say a word.

Olivia thought for a moment she may be sick, but she managed to control herself, control her disappointment, control the fury.

That was that, then. Luke would marry Kitty, and she would be a spinster here at Chalcroft, forever. How could she even think of marrying another when her heart was so firmly given to a man who neither deserved it, nor wanted it?

"Let the dancing begin!"

Her father's loud voice echoed over the babble of the guests, and his words were met with laughter and cheers. Everyone else was happy.

Olivia blinked back tears. Of course they were. They had not had their heart ripped out, right before their eyes. They did not have to wait for the announcement that would end their happiness. Would they announce it today—tonight?

The musicians struck up the opening notes, designed to gather together the dancers.

"Come on, Joy!" cried out Lucy in a fit of excitement, pulling Isabella with one hand and Maria with the other.

Laughing and teasing each other, the Fitzroy cousins stepped to the middle of the ballroom, which had now been vacated for the dancers. Gentlemen followed them, some Olivia knew, some she did not. Every single Fitzroy cousin was here. Even Harmony and Jemima were standing up with their husbands, though the latter looked a little pale.

And Kitty...Kitty was moving to join the line with Luke. Hand in hand.

Olivia swallowed, but try as she might, could not look away from the offending scene. Though it brought her nothing but misery, she watched as Luke released Kitty's hand as she took her place beside Isabella.

Nine Fitzroy sisters and cousins here tonight, and Olivia...Olivia was the only one not dancing.

The thought struck her painfully, and she wrapped her arms around her waist as though that would protect her.

No one had asked her. It was not just Luke who had not wished to dance with her, but no gentlemen at all.

There was still time, Olivia told herself hurriedly. Still time for someone to see her and desire her—or take pity on her—and then she could...

The musicians began their music, and the dance began. The eight Fitzroy cousins, and a woman Olivia did not recognize.

Nine ladies dancing.

Despite herself, despite knowing what pain it would cause her, Olivia moved slowly around the room to be closer to the dancers. To watch, to see just how much affection Kitty was able to draw out of Luke. To see what her sister had done to him that she had been unable to.

And yet...it was most strange. Though Kitty had managed to

gain the hand of the most handsome gentleman in the room, to Olivia's eyes, she did not look happy. There was a drawn, almost miserable expression on her face.

Had Luke told her, perhaps, of his betrayal? Olivia's shoulders tensed at the very idea, but it was possible. Had Luke just informed Kitty that he had also kissed her? Was there a tiff, a rift between the two lovers now he had made a full admission?

Yet as Olivia watched them, that idea did not make any sense. Luke looked more than happy; he looked triumphant. It was most incongruous, and Olivia could not make heads nor tales of it.

But the fact was—

"Olivia!" Luke said, the dance moving him closer to her, and his portion pausing while the dancers on either side of him took up the steps. "You are not dancing!"

Olivia glared. "No, it appears not."

"Well, why on earth not?" asked Luke, a little breathless from the dance, a grin on his face. "It's marvelous fun!"

And that was the last straw. The idea that he would say such a thing to her, knowing that she wished to dance with him, knowing how she felt about him, while he stood there, lying to her, teasing her about Kitty—it was too much.

Olivia knew she should say nothing. Knew she should maintain a dignified silence, one that all around her could respect—but she was pushed beyond endurance, and that was when her passion came out.

With no thought as to the people around them or who may hear her words, Olivia's glare became furious.

"How—how dare you speak to me like that, after what you have said and done," Olivia hissed under her breath, but Luke appeared astonished. "How dare you accept my attentions, tease me, tempt me along a path that I—and you were interested in Kitty all along!"

"Kitty—Katarina, you mean?" Luke said, eyes wide. "Olivia, you do not understand—"

"Oh, I think you will find that I understand perfectly," snapped Olivia, heat boiling in her blood. No one else could hear her over the music, but Luke continued to stare at her as though she was possessed. "What I do not think you understand is just how scandalous your behavior is—when I was going to—at least, perhaps. I should never have listened to you. I should never have let you—"

"Olivia, you have this all wrong," said Luke urgently, his eyes not leaving hers, even though the dance was now requiring his attention.

Olivia glanced over his shoulder to see whether Kitty was offended that she had stolen the attention of her gentleman—but she blinked. Kitty did not appear to be there anymore. Where on earth had she gone?

"—explain to your sister precisely what," Luke was saying, but Olivia spoke over him.

"I have no more to say on the matter, except that I will leave you to find your intended," Olivia said stiffly. "I have no wish to take up any more of your precious time."

"Precious time—intended? Olivia, wait!"

But Olivia did not wait. Turning on her heels and walking as quickly as she could in the opposite direction, she refused to let tears fall and refused to turn to see if Luke was following her. She hoped he wasn't. She hoped she never had to see him again.

CHAPTER SEVEN

Blind to where she was going, unable to think, only to feel, Olivia stormed through the crowds of people who were watching the nine ladies dancing.

She had to get away. Unsure precisely where away was, Olivia found to her displeasure that almost every room downstairs appeared to be full of guests.

"Ah, Miss Olivia! What a wonderful Christmas Eve ball your father has—"

"Your mother surely chose the decorations, and how beautiful they are! Tell me, where did she—"

"Olivia, wait!"

One voice rose above the rest; a strong, manly voice Olivia knew only too well. Refusing to allow herself to be halted by the warm greetings and questions of her parents' guests, Olivia pushed past them into the great hall, found no peace there and into the dining room, where food was piled on platters and more voices called to greet her—and still behind her was the one voice she had no wish to hear.

"Olivia, stop! Olivia!"

Heart pounding, Olivia knew one thing for certain; she would not stop. No matter how much Luke shouted, no matter how many heads turned to look at her, astonished as to why one of the Fitzroy girls was running away from that handsome gentleman—

Olivia would not stop.

But where could she go?

There was only one place the guests would not go for certain, and without a second thought, without considering that it was madness, without thinking whether or not Luke would follow her, Olivia strode across the room, threw open a door to the servants' corridor, and rushed down it.

The noise and chatter of the guests fell behind her, giving Olivia a moment to think over the frantic beating of her heart, but then—

"Olivia, will you just stop and listen to me!"

It had not occurred to her that Luke would be so bold as to follow her down the servants' corridor—but now Olivia was almost running, her heart pounding, breath tight in her lungs, and she knew she could not go back. The corridor was narrow, and the only person she would face if she turned back was Luke.

No, she had to go forward, had to somehow find solace in the kitchens. If she could ever find solace again.

Olivia burst into the kitchen, panting with the exertion, skirts flying.

"Miss Olivia!"

Cook turned to her in shock. He and a few of the other servants were seated around the wide kitchen table. Olivia was not surprised the servants looked astonished as they rose to their feet. She was, after all, dressed in a beautiful gown, and should really be in the ballroom, having the time of her life.

Instead, she was here, red faced, breathless, a few of her curls falling from her carefully placed pins, utterly heartbroken.

"Miss Olivia, what is it?" Cook said, taking a step toward her.

Olivia opened her mouth but with no idea what on earth she could say. How could she explain the predicament she had managed to find herself in? How would she ever admit to what she had allowed Luke to do to her—what she had said to him?

You make me warm, Luke. Hot. I want you to touch me, touch me with your fingers, and kiss me, and show me you want me as...as I want you."

"Olivia!" Luke stumbled into the kitchen just as breathless as she was. "Why didn't you wait when I...when I..."

Olivia saw, to her relief, that Luke's voice trailed away as he met the gazes of the servants who were all glaring at him. They did not need to be told. They could see from the very way that he had evidently been chasing her, just what had—or had not—occurred.

"Go away," Olivia said under her breath, turning to him with crimson cheeks.

"You have completely misunderstood, and I will make you understand," said Luke in a dark voice. "Everyone, out!"

Olivia turned to the servants. They would not abandon her, would they? They would not leave her to speak with Luke alone? It would risk her very reputation if she was permitted to be alone with Luke Kingsley.

Although, of course, she already had. Been alone with him, that was. And that, Olivia thought grimly, was where all of these problems started.

"No, stay," she said.

But there appeared a steely glint in Luke's eyes, and he glared at Cook. "I order you and everyone else, to leave. I must have five minutes alone with Miss Olivia. No one is to return to the kitchens until I give my permission."

Olivia almost laughed. Who did he think he was, giving orders here? This was Chalcroft for goodness' sake! The home of the Fitzroys for hundreds of years! A mere Kingsley could not step in here and start expecting to have his orders followed.

But her mouth fell open, not for the first time, as Cook gave a short bow and started to walk toward the door, the footmen and two maids following him.

"No—wait," Olivia said hastily, her heart pattering most painfully at the thought of a private conversation with Luke.

Five minutes alone with Luke? She would be forced to endure the full story of how he had fallen in love with Kitty; how they cared for each other, how he had not meant to lead her on, but now it was clear that it was Kitty he loved, beyond any other Fitzroy.

No, she would not suffer through that.

"I order you to stay!" she said, completely ineffectually.

For a reason she could not understand, the Fitzroy servants trooped out of the kitchen. Cook shut the door behind him, and Olivia was left in silence.

But she was not left alone.

"What about the food for the guests?" Olivia said, turning on him, aware that the food had already been served but unwilling to speak openly of the reason which tugged at her heartstrings. "I suppose you did not think of that when you stormed in here and—"

"Damn the food," said Luke succinctly.

Olivia gaped at him. He was mad. Mad for love—in love with Kitty.

It tore at her very soul. She was the most unfortunate woman who had ever lived. Had anyone ever endured such pain?

"I need to speak with you," said Luke, taking a step toward her. "And you would not be reasonable and listen to me in the ballroom, or the dining room, or anywhere else it seemed, but here. So you will stay here, and you will listen to me."

Olivia glared. "I will not."

Stepping away from him as swiftly as she could manage, Olivia attempted to reach the door—but Luke was too quick for her. He positioned himself between her and the door, and raised a quizzical eyebrow.

"I would have thought you, of all people, would want to hear what I am about to say," he said quietly. "You surprise me, Olivia."

"I—I surprise you!" Olivia could barely think, but she could laugh. "You are a fool, Luke Kingsley, of the finest degree. How could you think I would want to hear—you are mad!"

"Perhaps I am mad," said Luke in a low voice, not taking his gaze away from her face. "I had thought…had expected you to wish to hear what I had planned to say this evening. You had given me cause to think you would wish to hear it—"

"Cause!" Olivia scoffed as she turned her back on him, walking to the kitchen table and placing her hands upon it.

The cheek! The absolute audacity of the man! To think that he believed she had given him encouragement to speak to her about his affection of Kitty—it was too cruel.

Perhaps he enjoyed this. Perhaps this had been his plan all along, to tease her until she was within his power, and then to reveal that his affections lay elsewhere.

He was a cruel man—and yet she loved him. It was most unfair. The moment Christmas was over and the extended Fitzroy family had left for London and Bath, she would immediately be considering a plan of self-improvement.

"Yes, cause," came Luke's voice from behind her, and for some reason it cracked. There was deep emotion there, emotion Olivia did not wish to hear. "I thought you had made it clear that—damnit, Olivia, I thought we understood each other!"

"Oh, we do," said Olivia darkly, leaning against the kitchen table as she looked at him.

And in that moment, she was filled with absolute calm and resolve.

She was a Fitzroy. She may not like the situation she had found herself in, but it was one—partly—of her own making. And that meant she could unmake it.

"I understand you perfectly," Olivia said, allowing a little warmth back into her voice. "I have known you so well for so many years, Luke Kingsley, that sometimes I think it is you who does not understand. I saw how you looked at her."

"Yes, and—what?" Luke stared, confusion finally blotting the certainty on his features. "What do you mean, *her*?"

Olivia laughed. Well, if he wanted her to spell it out! "Katarina, of course!"

Luke fell against the door, still staring at her as though lost.

"Katarina."

"Yes, Katarina!" Olivia could not understand why he was making her say it again. Did he enjoy this sort of cruel torture? "I saw the way you looked at her—at the punch table, holding hands, and when you were dancing together…when are you going to make the announcement?"

Luke took a step toward her. "Announcement?"

Desperately wishing she was not leaning against the kitchen table as there was now nowhere to go, Olivia nodded. "Yes, announcement—or have you not formally asked for Katarina's hand yet?"

Silence rang out across the kitchen; silence except for the pain in Olivia's soul, which she was almost certain Luke would be able to hear.

And then he laughed.

He laughed. At her. It was unconscionable!

"You…you think I am in love with Katarina?"

Olivia hesitated. Until now she had been absolutely certain, it had seemed so obvious; but it was difficult to say so in the face of such blatant laughter.

"You…well, you asked her to dance with you," she said a little uncertainly.

Luke was shaking his head, his handsome features pulled into a smile. "You think every gentleman who asks a lady to dance wishes to propose marriage?"

"No, I am not a child!" said Olivia hotly.

"That you are not."

"And another thing," Olivia said, choosing to ignore that comment, though it brought heat to her face. "You were holding her hand—you made that other young man go away."

"Because she had no wish to dance with him," said Luke simply.

"Because she wished to dance with you!"

"Because she had something to discuss with me which she did not believe she could discuss with her sisters."

76

Olivia stared. Something…something Kitty needed to discuss but could not with her—or Isabella, who was admittedly far more understanding. What was it? There was something amiss, it seemed, between the Fitzroy sisters of Chalcroft…and she had not even noticed.

"Is she quite well?" she asked urgently.

Luke nodded. "Your care for her does you credit."

Olivia sniffed. The wooden table behind her felt solid, secure, giving her confidence. "If my care was as impressive as you say, she would not be going to you for help."

Luke shrugged, and Olivia's heart almost burst with pain, she loved him so much. "Well, I am not so sure about that. We will have to see."

Olivia nodded. She felt herself sagging against the kitchen table as relief started to course through her veins, relieving the tension in her shoulders and neck she had not even realized she was carrying.

Luke was not in love with Kitty.

The thought, small as it was, gave her great relief. He was not in love with her sister. It did not solve the ultimate problem of course, but…

There was a knowing smile on Luke's lips. "So you thought I was in love with your sister."

Olivia flushed. "No, I—I thought…"

There was nothing she could say that would remove her from this embarrassing situation, so she allowed her voice to fade away. If only he wasn't looking at her like that. Like he was a cat who had gained complete ownership of the cream.

He took a step closer, and Olivia was uncomfortably conscious that Luke was now but a few feet away.

"Why did that idea upset you so?"

"Because you know full well that I am in love with you!"

Olivia clapped her hands over her mouth, but it was too late. The words were said; words that appeared to echo around the kitchen, reminding Luke over and over again of the words she had hidden for so long, but had now escaped her.

"I am in love with you...I am in love with you..."

Olivia dropped her gaze and examined the hem of her skirts.

Well, that was it. She would never be able to stay in Luke's presence again, certainly not alone, and definitely not with her family present. It was all over. She had utterly embarrassed herself, and sadly, not for the first time. He must think her a complete fool.

But when Olivia finally managed to lift her gaze and look at Luke, there was a smile on his face.

Not a wry one. Not a rueful one, or mischievous one... There was no wicked glint in his eyes, nor cheeky tone in his voice when he spoke.

Instead, Luke looked...strange. "Why...why did you not say before?"

There you go, Olivia thought dully. The absolute worst has happened. Luke Kingsley feels sorry for you.

"Why do you think?" she said with a shrug, clutching at the kitchen table behind her as though that would support her through this conversation. "I am no fool, Luke. You have made it very clear that you...you appreciated my kisses, but you desire nothing more. Nothing permanent, I mean. I may love you but you...you do not want...want that from me."

Olivia could hardly believe she was speaking so openly—but it was what happened next that truly took the breath from her lungs.

"Oh, Olivia," said Luke quietly, taking another step toward her so that they were now mere inches apart. "Olivia, you could not have that more wrong."

More wrong? What did he mean? Surely he could not mean that...

"Nothing," Luke said softly, "could be further from the truth."

Olivia swallowed. "N-Nothing?"

And now he was standing right before her, his chest pressed

up against hers, and Olivia had nowhere else to go but also had no desire to be elsewhere. Not with Luke here, the two of them together, alone.

As she had desperately wanted them to be.

"You do not seem to believe my words," said Luke with a wicked look. "Let me see if my actions can speak louder."

And he was kissing her—kissing her far more wildly than he had in the drawing room, that night she had discovered him downstairs—and Olivia was kissing him, kissing him as passionately as she could muster.

For he must care for her, mustn't he?

"You do not want…want that from me."

"Olivia, you could not have that more wrong."

He loved her. Olivia knew it, felt it in the way he pulled her to him, believed it in the way he quickly parted her lips with his tongue, his fingers not at her waist but on her bottom, cupping her to him in a way that made Olivia tingle all over.

"Luke…"

"Olivia, I have wanted this for so long," Luke said breathlessly, pulling away from her only to say those words before kissing her neck, trailing kisses down from her ear to her décolletage, and lower…

Olivia gasped as his breath and lips brushed the very tops of her breasts, her back arching to give him more of her, more of everything she was.

"Luke…"

Perhaps it was hearing his name again that made Luke halt, but as he straightened up and looked in her eyes, Olivia could see the lust and the desire—and something else—

"I want you," he said in a jagged voice.

"And I want you."

"Do not misunderstand me," Luke said quietly, looking searchingly into Olivia's eyes. "What I ask…what I want of you is everything a lady can give a man. I do not ask it lightly of you, Olivia…dear Olivia…and I wish you to consider it seriously before you—"

Olivia did not permit him to continue. Crushing her lips against his, and feeling her heart thunder, she moved slightly out of his arms—but not far.

Lifting her bottom onto the table, Olivia shuffled back slightly, spread her knees apart, and breaking the kiss with Luke, which made him groan, causing a tingling thrill to pass through her, she met his gaze. She did not break his gaze as she slowly lifted her skirts above her ankles…above her calves…to her knees…

"Christ, Olivia," said Luke in a croaky voice.

Olivia gloried in the power she had over him as she slowly lifted her skirts above her knees to her thighs, revealing the light underwear she was wearing. Revealing herself to him. Revealing everything she was to the man she loved.

"We…we…anyone could come in and find us," said Luke weakly, though his eyes shone with desire, his hands now on her knees, as though he wished to touch more of her but could not bring himself to.

Olivia smiled. The very thought had rushed through her mind, but in a strange way, it made the entire experience even more exciting. The thought that they could be caught at any moment…it was intoxicating.

"I know," she whispered, lying back slowly onto the wooden kitchen table and arching her back. "So, what are you waiting for?"

Luke groaned and moved between her legs—but not as Olivia had expected. She knew a little about the act of love and was certain that his manhood would need to enter her—but instead of pulling off his breeches, he was getting down on bended knee.

"Luke, what are you—Luke!"

It was all Olivia could do not to scream. Luke was gently kissing down her inner thigh, his fingers gently brushing against her, against the part of her between her legs, and it felt wonderful, and warm, and tantalizing. As though it promised of more to come.

"I...I don't know—"

"Trust me," said Luke from the floor at the edge of the table. "I want to kiss you, Olivia. Would you like that? Would you like my tongue inside you?"

Olivia quivered on the kitchen table. "Yes."

She had only spoken in a whisper, hardly brave enough to think the answer let alone say it. What did she think she was doing?

But it felt right, as well as wicked. This was Luke—there was no one else she wanted to share this with.

"Oh, God, you are so beautiful," moaned Luke as he slid a finger underneath her underwear and slowly brought it down her legs, allowing it to drop to the floor.

Olivia shivered, the sensation of bareness overwhelming—but nothing could have prepared her for what happened next.

His lips—oh, his lips were on her! Olivia squirmed, but Luke placed his hands lovingly yet strongly on her hips, keeping her still—just as his tongue entered her.

"Luke!"

Olivia tried not to shout too loudly, knew if they were too loud, then someone would come running, no matter what Luke had told them—but she could not keep silent, it was too much!

The warmth of his tongue, the way it moved inside her, it was too much. Olivia's eyelashes fluttered as she lost herself in the delicate slow movements, as Luke's hands lovingly caressed her hips and her inner thighs, and Olivia shivered with pleasure.

For it was pleasure. As his tongue gained pace, Olivia moaned again, the pleasure building in her, building a heat she did not understand, but it was the same ache she had felt when Luke had kissed her against the drawing room wall, and it was him she needed, needed for her release.

"More, more, yes," Olivia found herself moaning, unable to help herself, unable to resist the temptation to speak out her passion, and it seemed to spur Luke on, so she moaned again. "More, yes!"

She could do nothing but cry out his name as the crest of pleasure she was riding suddenly peaked, overwhelming her, spinning her mind and her heart as her whole body pulsed on the kitchen table with the ecstasy she had never before known.

It was several moments before Olivia subsided. When she finally felt able to open her eyes, Luke was standing between her legs, something akin to devotion on his face.

"Olivia Fitzroy, you are magnificent," he said jerkily. "Christ, I thought…and you let me…"

Olivia smiled weakly up at him. "I would let you do that to me every day of my life."

Luke chuckled as he fumbled at the buttons at the front of his breeches. "Careful, I might hold you to that—now, I want to hear you cry my name again. Ready?"

Olivia nodded, hardly aware of what she could possibly be ready for, and arched her back with shock and pleasure as Luke pressed his manhood into her.

Though expecting pain, Olivia was surprised to find there was none. There was a pressure, yes, and a sense of being full, full to bursting—but it was rather pleasant.

"You look beautiful, Olivia," said Luke quietly. "I'll… I'll do my best to bring you pleasure again, but I may just lose control."

Olivia looked up into his face, and knew he loved her. What else could he feel to do this to her, to show her this sort of pleasure, to give her such sensations?

"Love me," she whispered.

Luke groaned and held her hips once more, but this time not so that she did not buck under the unexpected carnality, but so that he could have a firm grip.

Watching in amazement, and then in barely controlled pleasure, Olivia saw him move slightly out of her and then into her, causing a ripple of ecstasy to move through her. This was it. This was everything. This was the connection she had craved, the completion of the desire she had tasted as he had kissed her against the drawing room wall.

This was their moment to share, what a lady and gentleman could, but not in a bed, like an old married couple—but here, where their lust had found them.

And she wanted more. Dear God, she wanted more.

"Do that again," Olivia said. "Please, Luke, I want—I want you."

Luke groaned again as he repeated the action, thrusting into her with a little more pressure. "I have wanted to do this to you since the moment I arrived here this Christmas."

Olivia arched her back, trying to move her hips in time with his own, extending the pleasure. "And I wanted you, too."

Luke moaned as he started to increase the rhythm. "I wanted to hear you say you wanted me."

"And I wanted you to kiss me."

"And I wanted you to touch me."

"And I wanted—oh Luke, yes, harder!" Olivia could hardly help herself, knew the words she was saying were disgraceful, that only a harlot would think these things let alone say them, but she could not help it. She was one with Luke, one with the man she loved, and she had opened herself to him, and she wanted him to have everything, all of her.

"Love me, Luke!" Olivia cried out, the pressure of the aching pleasure building up inside her so deeply that it was all she could do to grip the edges of the table, her fingers scraping the wood.

"Olivia!"

It was enough. Finally pushed beyond the edge of endurance, Luke pounded into her, exploding himself—

And then Luke had fallen on top of her, unable to hold his own weight after such pleasure.

And Olivia clutched him to her, and knew she would never be the same again.

CHAPTER EIGHT

O LIVIA HAD NO memory of making her way from the kitchen to the servants' corridor. She did not remember walking along the servants' corridor, nor finding her way up the back staircase, which led to the upper floor, where the family slept.

She could not recall letting herself onto the main corridor, walking down it, and finding the door to her own bedchamber. Olivia could not remember removing her gown, placing it carefully on the chair, and creeping into bed.

The room had been empty when she had retreated upstairs. Isabella must have come in at some point, but Olivia must have slept through it.

Yet despite having no memory of these events, Olivia was certain they must have happened. They must have; otherwise, how else was she able to wake up on Christmas morning, the smell of snow in the air, in her own bed, in her nightgown?

Olivia blinked. This was her bed, wasn't it?

Olivia leaned back against her pillows, but her mind was just as anxious, just as lost. Just as shocked at herself for what she had, in a moment of weakness, of desperation, allowed herself to do.

"I have wanted to do this to you since the moment I arrived here this Christmas."

"And I wanted you, too."

"I wanted to hear you say you wanted me."

Olivia raised a hand to her cheeks and felt the scalding warmth. Well they might burn. She had done precisely what no woman should be doing until she was wed—and even then, she was not entirely sure that was precisely how a respectably married woman was supposed to make love!

"And I wanted you to kiss me."

"And I wanted you to touch me."

"And I wanted—oh Luke, yes, harder!"

Olivia closed her eyes for a moment, allowing herself to seep into the memories, even as her heart rebelled. The sensation of the hard wooden table beneath her and the softness of Luke's touch above her.

The pleasure she had felt, but more than that, the safety she had felt. The desire she felt for him, and the desire she felt flowing from him as he kissed her, as he made love to her.

There was such a sense of completeness…one that Olivia had never known. No wonder people liked doing it, she thought to herself wryly in the cold silence of the morning. No wonder ladies were tempted to lose their innocence before they were wed.

It was a miracle, really, that anyone reached their wedding day with their innocence intact, if that was what they were missing.

But though it was delectable and delicious to think of such wonderful things, Olivia sadly forced herself to cease recalling them.

Because she couldn't. She shouldn't. It was wrong, somehow, wrong to enjoy such things, to enjoy the touches of a gentleman like Luke Kingsley—from any gentleman!

And besides, it was not as though he had made her any promises, was it?

The thought rushed through her mind most painfully, but Olivia caught at it, astonished she had not considered this before.

Olivia drew her knees up and wrapped her arms around them, as though that would prevent her from having said any words to him. To Luke.

He had not said that he loved her. True, he had made love to her...but even Olivia, in the headiness of her passion, and now in the cold light of morning, knew it was not the same thing.

Sighing heavily, she allowed her legs to straighten, and wondered what on earth the day could hold for her now. It was impossible to consider how she would be able to look Luke in the eyes, now that he had...well.

Tasted her. Kissed her, thrust into her, losing himself to the pleasuring of her.

Olivia was no longer cold. Though the room was still freezing, ice patterns painted on the window panes, she felt remarkably hot and uncomfortable.

It was too late to feel regret now, she told herself. What was done was done, and there was no possibility of trying to change it. She would simply have to hold her head up high and remind herself that unless she or Luke revealed the truth to anyone, surely no one would be able to guess just by looking at them.

"You look different."

Olivia almost fell out of bed, she was so surprised. Isabella was grinning at her, lying on her side in the bed on the opposite side of the room.

"Wh-What do you mean?" Olivia said, doing a terrible impression of someone who was utterly at peace and calm in their surroundings.

How was it possible for her sister to notice that something was different, and so quickly, too? It was ridiculous! It was impossible...wasn't it?

"I don't know, you just look...different," said Isabella with a yawn. "Can't a sister notice that another sister looks odd?"

Olivia smiled weakly. "I suppose there is no law against it."

Resisting the urge to rise from her snug bed to look into the looking glass, to see precisely whether there was anything different about her face that she could spot, Olivia instead merely smiled. "Merry Christmas."

"Goodness, so it is," said Isabella with another yawn. "You

know, I do not believe I got into bed before one o'clock in the morning—you had a much better idea, coming up earlier."

Olivia said nothing. Well, if that was what her sisters thought, that was far better than the potential alternative. In hindsight, that their father had invited so many people. It appeared her absence for the majority of the ball had gone unnoticed.

"I didn't see much of Kitty either," remarked Isabella, sitting up and leaning against a pillow. "Was she with you?"

Olivia swallowed before she spoke. "No, I did not see much of her."

Well, it was not entirely a lie, was it? She had seen a little of Kitty and had no wish to give any explanation as to her actual location.

But what would she say if Isabella kept asking these questions? How was she to explain where she was—and who she was with—without lying?

Thankfully, Isabella did not seem particularly interested in the goings on of her older sister. "Well, I think it was a remarkably pleasant ball, one of our best. Mama outdid herself with the decorations, and even Papa's exuberance did not overwhelm everyone."

Olivia nodded without saying anything. If there was anything she could trust in this moment, it was her silence. Words would surely risk betraying her.

"Come on then," sighed Isabella, pushing back the covers and dropping her feet onto the floor. "We had better get dressed."

It took almost half an hour for them to be ready to go down. Isabella was finished almost within ten minutes, but then she rarely gave much thought to her apparel and looks—Olivia rarely did herself.

Except for today. Today, she wanted to ensure she was absolutely perfect. Quite what perfect looked like, on the other hand, was utterly beyond her...

"Come on, you are taking forever!" moaned Isabella, leaning against the wall by the door. "I'll go down without you if you are going to linger for the rest of time!"

"What nonsense," said Olivia with a wry smile. "I just cannot decide between—"

"Both are fine," said Isabella.

Olivia laughed and felt a little of the tension in her shoulders dissipate. She should not be so frightened of seeing Luke, should she?

No, she was being ridiculous. Luke would say nothing, she would say nothing, and at the first opportunity, she would find a moment to speak with Luke and ascertain precisely what his intentions were toward her.

Something she should have done before she lifted her skirts in that outrageous way, but there it was...

Olivia lifted the pearl necklace up in one hand, and a golden chain with a locket in the other. "I just cannot decide."

What would Luke prefer?

"Then wear both!" said Isabella, apparently pushed beyond all endurance. "Or neither, 'tis all the same to me. I'm going downstairs. I'm starving."

Without another word, Isabella rushed through the door, slamming it behind her.

She always was so impatient, thought Olivia as she lifted first the pearls, then the gold locket against her neck. She had no idea that her sister was about to see the man to whom she had given her innocence.

With a broad smile, primarily from relief, Olivia placed both necklaces down on the toilette table and decided to go without. She was not attempting to impress anyone, after all. Luke was not going to be at Chalcroft much longer today.

She could worry about impressing him tomorrow.

Still, Olivia hardly walked downstairs with a spring in her step. The whole world seemed changed now, a sense of difference between her and her sisters. Separating them. Keeping them apart.

She felt more akin to Harmony and Jemima, who both greeted her with smiles as she entered the breakfast room, than anyone else. They at least understood what it was to share oneself with a gentleman; to share everything one was.

Not that she could ever talk to them about it. Everyone was there, all the Fitzroys except Katarina, for some reason, and Luke.

Olivia allowed her breathing to slow a touch. He was not here. She had time to regain her composure. Even if her cheeks were attempting to betray her.

"Goodness, that blaze is impressive," she said airily. "Our bedchamber was freezing, wasn't it Isabella?"

"Oh, I see you have finally decided to grace us with your presence," Isabella said with a grin.

Joy snorted. "Perfecting your hair, Olivia?"

"She couldn't decide what necklace to wear," said Isabella with a roll of her eyes, before Olivia could say anything. "And yet you wore neither! What a waste of time!"

"You look a little unwell, Jemima," said Harmony quietly. "Are you quite well?"

Olivia watched Jemima glance at her husband beside her. Hugh smiled and took his wife's hand, but said nothing.

"No," whispered Harmony. "No, you're not."

"I am," said Jemima, quite confusingly to Olivia's mind. "We only found out just before coming here, we did not wish to overshadow—"

"—going to have to do something about it," her Uncle Arthur was saying with a sad expression, despite it being Christmas Day. Olivia could see he was holding a letter in his hand. "Arabella sounded quite miserable in her letter, and so, of course, I wrote back to her to explain—"

"Has anyone seen Kitty?" asked Maria softly.

The hubbub of the room quieted as every eye turned to the youngest Chalcroft Fitzroy, who blushed most heartily at all the attention.

"I do not think so," said their father airily as he poured himself a cup of tea. "Good morning, Olivia, and happy Christmas."

"Happy Christmas, Papa," Olivia said warmly, stepping across the room to hug him from behind as he sat. "And while I have you, I wished to ask you—"

"I only mention it," piped up little Maria, "because...because Kitty did not come to bed last night."

The room fell entirely silent. Olivia glanced at her father, whose forehead had crinkled into concern.

"What do you mean, did not come to bed last night?" he repeated slowly.

Maria said, "That is all. She did not come to bed. She was not there when I went upstairs, or when I woke up—"

"But that does not signify anything, surely," said Harmony, the family's natural peacekeeper. "She could have come to bed later than you and risen earlier."

"Perhaps," admitted Maria. "But it is unlike Kitty to even attempt to make her bed, and...well...I would say it has not been slept in."

"I am sure she is fine."

Olivia looked around. Luke had entered the room, precisely when she was not sure, and his presence reminded her instantly of the lovemaking they had shared only hours before.

Her gaze met his, and she knew he was thinking of it, too. Would their looks betray them? Could someone see in her eyes the desire she felt for him?

Olivia looked away quickly.

"You seem rather certain of that, Kingsley, for someone who has little in the way of information," William Fitzroy said, rising to his feet. "Where could she be?"

"I only meant—"

"Do not concern yourself, Papa," said Olivia, placing a calming hand on his arm. Of course, Kitty would make it impossible for her to talk to their father about removing Luke for a short time. Even in her absence, Kitty was a nuisance!

"I really would like to find her before we have breakfast and open presents, and the like," said her Papa easily. "I suppose no one has seen her this morning?"

Olivia and the rest of the Fitzroy family looked around at each other. Fitzroy cousins were shrugging, evidently at a loss.

"Well, who saw her last?" asked Leonora, a strange tightness to her voice Olivia had never heard before.

"Papa," said Olivia softly.

It had been her hope to snatch a few minutes of conversation with him; merely enough to explain that Luke's continued presence here was starting to become...untenable. That he would need to be farmed out to some other family, where he could dance with their daughters, or open presents, or anything like that.

Anything to give Olivia a few hours to think. To be without his constant presence.

Even without looking at him, she could feel the heat of his gaze on the back of her neck. Why was he looking at her like that?

"—be concerned, a very cold night," Lucy was muttering to her sister. "If she was out of doors the entire—"

"Out of doors!" Olivia's mother looked at Lucy, then around the room. "Do we think that is possible?"

Lucy thoughtlessly shrugged. "Well, if she is not inside—but I am sure it is nothing to be concerned about."

"Not be concerned? My daughter is missing!"

"Missing is such a strong word," Olivia's Papa replied, who had risen, too, with a fearful expression on his face. "Mislaid, I would say is the best term at this moment."

"But should we look for her?" asked Jemima, looking instinctively to her husband Hugh who had also risen from his chair.

"A simple search of the house and grounds would not be too difficult to organize," Hugh said quietly. "With minimal fuss, of course."

Until that moment, Olivia had almost forgotten that Jemima had married a soldier. Yes, well, if they could deal with Kitty, then she could speak with her father.

"Papa," Olivia said quietly by his side.

He looked at her, brow furrowed. "You have some idea where Kitty could be?"

"Kitty—no," said Olivia rather dejectedly. "No, I wished to ask you a small favor."

"Well, cannot you see that I am a little preoccupied in this moment?" Her father uncharacteristically snapped.

Olivia stepped back, stung. It was not her fault that Katarina Fitzroy was an absolute fool. For all they knew, she had merely slept elsewhere! There were plenty of rooms in Chalcroft, plenty of places to curl up exhausted after a ball. There was no reason to believe that—

"A search, then," said her Papa to Hugh. "You can round up the troops?"

"Don't you worry, sir, I will soon have the servants marching to my drum," said Hugh with a brief smile. "You leave it to me."

Perhaps this would give her a chance to speak with her father alone.

But it was not to be.

"No, no, she is my daughter, I will come with you," said her Papa with a heavy sigh. "I should have known a Fitzroy Christmas could not continue without some sort of incident."

"We do not even know if it is an incident yet," said Esther, fairly. "She may have just...made her bed."

Katarina's three sisters shared a look. That seemed most unlikely.

"Kingsley, I am sure I can count on your support," said Hugh briskly. "And you, Navarre."

Harmony's husband David rose, murmuring words that sounded like, "Of course, happy to help."

But Luke did not move. "Actually, before I assist in any rescue mission, I need to speak to Olivia. Alone."

The entire room stared first at him, and then at Olivia. The weight of their gazes seemed to oppress her. Olivia was astonished that she did not take a seat as they all stared at her.

She swallowed. What did Luke think he was doing? Why did he want to draw even more attention to them?

"Alone?" she repeated.

Why did Luke have to smile like that? "Yes, alone."

The moment hung between them, perfectly balanced, and Olivia felt the tension in her shoulders grow.

Well, that would at least clear up a few things that she had been too overcome with carnality last night to discuss.

"Yes. Fine, well, I am sure that this conversation will not take long—and then I will return, Papa, and wish to speak with you."

Her father nodded, dismissing her with a wave of his hand. "Yes, yes, a discussion—but first we must find Kitty. Is it possible she went outside and got lost in the dark?"

"Lost? Here, at Chalcroft?" Even Maria's voice was incredulous.

Isabella shook her head as Luke stepped across the room toward Olivia. "No, she knows this place as we all do, perfectly, in daylight or night. What about…"

She continued talking, but Olivia was unsure precisely what she was saying. Luke had reached her side and allowed his fingers to gently graze hers.

It was as though a lightning bolt shot through her. Even here, standing with almost all her family, Olivia only felt alive when she was close by Luke. She was a fool. She had allowed herself to act the fool, and now he presumably wanted to tell her that he would not tell anyone about her outburst.

"You make me warm, Luke. Hot. I want you to touch me, touch me with your fingers, and kiss me, and show me you want me as…as I want you."

"Come on," murmured Luke softly, trying to take Olivia's hand in his. She pulled away. "The drawing room."

Olivia nodded mutely and followed him. Now to have one of the most difficult conversations of her life.

CHAPTER NINE

T HE DOOR CLOSED behind them, and Olivia immediately felt strangely trapped in the drawing room, despite its large size.

The fire was lit, burning brightly in the grate, throwing orangey amber light across the room and its multitude of Christmas decorations. It appeared that whatever decorations had been left at the end of decorating the house had been permitted to explode here; there were so many candles, Olivia felt as though she was in a church. Ribbons festooned over the portraits and landscapes. There was holly and ivy all along the curtain rail, making it almost impossible for the maids to draw the curtains, and there were even a few balls coated in silver paper around the door.

Also on the door, now Olivia came to look at it, was a wreath. A wreath she recognized.

She swallowed.

"You do that so well."

"You are not so bad yourself."

"I don't want to force myself onto your company, you know. I just…we were always good friends, you and I."

This entire Christmas was supposed to be about family, about her family.

She had not wanted Luke here, yet at the same time, she desperately had. She loved him. She belonged to him, Olivia knew that now. There was not a single other gentleman who would possess her heart as he now possessed it. There was nothing she could do to cut the ties between them.

"So," said Luke, jolting Olivia from her reverie. "How did you sleep?"

He was leaning against an armchair as he spoke, that mischievous grin Olivia knew and loved so well on his face. He looked so at ease, Olivia could not help but feel a little envious.

How was it that he could appear so calm, so collected? Was his heart not thumping wildly in his chest, as hers did in her own?

Was he not continuously revisited by memories of...of what they shared together?

"You look beautiful, Olivia. I'll...Christ, I'll do my best to bring you pleasure again, but I may just lose control."

Olivia's jaw tightened, and she attempted to control herself. She needed to speak and speak plainly. She had never had a problem with speaking openly to Luke before. So much of her childhood and youth had been with him, open and honest and artless.

But that had all changed. Everything had changed, and now she had to explain to this handsome, dazzling man just what she was thinking. If she could even understand herself.

"We...we should not have done that."

Luke frowned slightly. "I beg your pardon? You should not have slept? You think your sister Katarina's idea better, to drive her family wild with panic and fear?"

"You know that is not what I meant," said Olivia sharply.

Luke grinned. "I like it when you shout at me."

Was there ever such an intolerable gentleman? Olivia did not believe so. What a shame he was wrapped up in the face of the most handsome man she had ever known.

Olivia shook her head, as though that would dislodge the thoughts that shot through her mind. She needed to stay focused—she needed to make sure she did not entirely lose herself!

She had to have this conversation. She had to say the words

that were bubbling up in her mind, as yet unspoken, but necessary. Even if they would hurt her just as much as they would hurt him.

"We...we should not have done what we did," Olivia said, lowering her voice as though her family may hear her through the door and across the great hall. "Last night. In...in the kitchen."

Heat blossomed across her body at the mere reference of what they shared together, what they had done. The line they had transgressed, the scandalous thing they had done. If they had been caught...

Luke stared. "You...you cannot possibly mean that."

"I do," said Olivia stiffly. Well, he was almost right. If he had declared himself for her, if he had asked for her hand, then perhaps all this guilt would not be seeping through her veins. But he had not, and so they had. "We shouldn't have done it."

Luke took a step toward her. "But I don't—"

His voice broke off as he turned to the window. Olivia looked there, too; it was impossible not to. From this angle, they could see a slightly disheveled looking Katarina walk up the drive, still wearing her evening gown from the ball the night before. Her hair was down, all thought of pins forgotten, and—was that straw in her hair?

Olivia ignored Luke, stepping past him to reach the window. He was not too far behind her, his presence warm and comforting as he leaned forward to look.

"Kitty," breathed Olivia.

"And not alone, either," said Luke wryly.

Just behind her strode a man Olivia recognized, but could not place. But that did not matter. A huge gaggle of people had spilled out of the house, her father was leading the way.

"Katarina Fitzroy, what have you done!"

Her Papa's shout was so loud, Olivia could hear it through the mullioned windows of Chalcroft's old glass.

Whatever response he received was lost, however, for Katarina spoke without shouting. The Fitzroy cousins spread out across the drive, encircling Kitty, and Olivia could see her no more.

"Well, well," breathed Luke. Olivia shivered as the warmth of his breath on the back of her neck made her tremble. "She got her man after all."

Olivia turned around immediately, then hastily stepped to the side. Luke was right behind her, and as she turned, she had brushed up against him in a way that was far too delicious.

"What do you mean, got her man?" Olivia said sharply. "You—you know all about this, don't you?"

Perhaps her tone was a little aggressive.

Luke put up his hands in surrender. "Only a snippet, I promise you, and most of that I inferred. Katarina actually told me very little."

Olivia glanced back outside the window but could see nothing but the gaggle of Fitzroys. She could hardly work out within herself what she was most frustrated by; that she was not a part of the situation, not knowing whether Kitty was quite safe, unsure why her sister had felt unable to come to her in the first place—or frustrated at the man before her, who seemed so relaxed at the idea that Kitty could have...that she, too, last night might have...

"You," said Olivia slowly. "You and me...I do not think...we should not have done it."

Luke watched her in silence, clearly patient enough to wait until she found the words, which she was grateful for. Olivia was not sure there were words.

How did one explain to the person you loved, that you adored beyond all others, that she should not have given herself to him?

"I wanted you," Olivia said slowly, her face only pinking slightly as she spoke of her passion. "And you wanted me, and in that moment, it was glorious, and wonderful, and—"

"It was rather, wasn't it?" said Luke with a grin.

Olivia quickly stepped away. "Not this time," she said with a warning finger and a wry smile. "Damnit, Luke, you make it so—so difficult to say what I think!"

Luke shrugged, his charming smile only perfected by a lock of hair that fell over his eyes. "What can I say?"

"You can say nothing!" Olivia said, perhaps a little more sternly than she meant.

Luke halted his steps toward her, and looked at her seriously for the first time that day. "Olivia, I...I meant no harm yesterday. I would not have done anything. I did not do anything that I thought you would refuse."

"I know that," said Olivia softly.

Oh, it was all going wrong. How could she explain it to him?

"Come." Luke sat in an armchair beside the fire, crackling away merrily. "Sit."

Olivia gave him a look. What did he want with her now? What sort of plans did he have for her? Those two armchairs were close, close enough to touch.

"You do not have to be suspicious," said Luke. "I promise, I won't touch you—and that is a great deal, coming from me, because I would much rather have you naked under me than clothed opposite. Come."

He sat down with a flourish, tucking his coat tails behind him as he did so, and Olivia managed to step over to the fireplace and sit in the armchair opposite him without falling over, which she thought was rather impressive.

"I would much rather have you naked under me than clothed opposite me."

Olivia shivered as she arranged her skirts, despite the warmth of the fire. What was it about Luke that managed to get under her skin so entirely and completely? How did he manage to do that?

How did he have such a power over her, even before they had made love?

"Right," said Luke with a small smile. "You wish to speak, and I think you have much to say. Do not be afraid, Olivia. We have…we have shared much, we have spoken openly about our desires. Do not you think I would wish to hear your fears, too?"

Olivia took a deep breath. His words were so comforting, so honest. She could see the honesty in his eyes.

He cared for her, cared in a way she did not understand. But he was right. They had shared much, and it was ridiculous that she was now afraid of speaking openly before him.

While the rest of the Fitzroy family concerned themselves with whatever mischief Kitty had managed to get herself into, Olivia knew this was the best moment to have a direct conversation with Lord Luke Kingsley.

If she could find the words.

"Luke," she said finally.

"Olivia," he said with a grin.

Olivia frowned, and he nodded, leaning back as though showing her he was willing to listen.

"Last night was…oh, my goodness, it was wonderful," Olivia said slowly, her stomach twisting at the mere memory of what Luke's tongue could do to her. "But do you not see how it was wrong?"

"No," said Luke quietly. "No, when I think back to those moments we shared, everything within it feels beautiful. Almost perfect. As though my entire life led up to that moment, and I was so grateful. So honored to share that with you."

Olivia flushed and looked down at her hands. "You don't feel…well, shame? I mean, I know a lady is not supposed to do anything like that."

"Certainly not on a kitchen table, no."

"Luke Kingsley!"

He laughed gently with no malice. "Well, I cannot help it! I cannot regret what we shared, what we created together. You think that…Olivia, this may surprise you, but has it ever occurred to you that that was the first experience for me, too?"

Olivia's jaw dropped. Luke was looking at her a little abashed now, as though he had admitted something truly secret.

His first experience? She could not believe it. A gentleman who knew precisely how to touch her, to tease her, to please her...

Though she had not given it much thought, in truth, and though she did not like the idea of sharing him with someone, anyone, Olivia had unconsciously thought—she now realized— that she was one in a line of ladies who Luke had ravished.

But he was looking at her now with the shyness of the boy she had first fallen in love with all those years ago. When they had been but twelve or thirteen, and started to realize that they were different.

"Luke Kingsley," Olivia breathed. "Are...are you in earnest?"

"You think I would share that with anyone else?" Luke said lightly. "You think I would wish to sully the memories I intended to make with you, by practicing with someone else? Perhaps you do not know me as well as you think."

Olivia swallowed. Perhaps she did not. She had assumed a man as handsome, as worldly, as Luke Kingsley would have had plenty of...well, to use his own word, practice.

But he had not. She could see that now, see it in the way that he held himself, a little more stiffly than appeared comfortable. Just as she had given herself to him for the first time, exploring, not knowing precisely what was going to happen next...

So had he. He had saved himself for her.

Olivia cleared her throat. "So...so you did not decide to make love to me because you merely desired me? Or felt sorry for me?"

Pure astonishment flushed across Luke's face. "You think I would do that?"

"I don't know," said Olivia quickly. "I just—after seeing you dance with Kitty—"

"You have got to put that out of your head, you know," Luke interjected. "I would never have danced with her to save her the indignation of dancing with that cad who approached her, if I had known it would upset you so."

Olivia smiled weakly. It did seem silly, now she came to think about it. A gentleman could dance with several ladies in one night; it did not mean, as he had said yesterday, that he was intending to propose marriage to any of them.

"You know, I like that we still have much to learn about each other," said Luke thoughtfully as he examined her. "We have known each other for so long, you and I, I honestly thought there was perhaps nothing new to learn. And when we are married—"

"When?" interrupted Olivia, heart pounding, fingers clenching the arms of her chair. "Wh-What do you—when?"

Luke grinned. "You did not think I would make love to you on a kitchen table, make you cry out my name, and then not propose marriage in the morning?"

Olivia flushed.

"Dear God—what sort of a cad do you think I am?" laughed Luke. "Olivia Fitzroy, you scandalous hussy, did it not occur to you that you could propose to me!"

"Luke!" Olivia exclaimed, but she could say no more, he was laughing too much—and eventually, she joined him.

Well, he was right. There was nothing stopping her from proposing marriage to him—and now that he had spoken of when they were married, there appeared to be little question that he did wish to marry her.

And yet...

Olivia's laughter faded as she looked at him. She loved him so much, so much it hurt. There was an ache in her chest that was not quite healed yet, and that was because despite his lovemaking and his words of affection this morning, there were certain words that Luke Kingsley had not spoken to her.

He had not said that he loved her.

And she could not force him. Olivia had no desire to make him say them; those sorts of words had to be freely spoken to have any true meaning.

"You still do not trust me."

Olivia laughed awkwardly as Luke examined her with a wry expression. "It is not that! It is...well. You have seen so much more of the world than I have, traveled, been to university, lived in Town...I admit, I find it difficult to believe that of all the women you have met, you would...would choose me."

It was difficult to say, but Olivia pushed herself beyond the point of comfort. A log crackled in the fire, shifting and throwing up sparks.

Well, she had spoken—and Luke did not look as though he was about to disappear.

Quite to the contrary, he leaned forward, reached for her hands, and then just before their fingertips brushed, he pulled back.

"Damn," he said under his breath. "I promised not to touch you."

Olivia did not think, she merely acted. Leaning forward herself, she took Luke's large, heavy hands in hers.

"I didn't," she said lightly.

Luke chuckled, shaking his head. "And you wonder why...Olivia, I have danced with all nine ladies here at one time or another. Your father has always been so generous in inviting me here, and I wondered sometimes whether he knew that I..."

His voice trailed away as Olivia looked deep into his eyes. There was such rich emotion there, a depth to him that she had never quite seen before. Perhaps he had never before shared it.

"None of them, not one, make me feel the way you do," said Luke softly. "I thought you understood that."

Olivia shook her head slightly. "No, you have never said that—"

"I did not think you needed words," said Luke. His voice was low, yet urgent. "Do you remember last Easter, when I came to visit for two weeks? We danced at a ball, and you laughed when I asked you to dance a second time, and I said..."

Olivia smiled bashfully. She could remember the moment as though it was yesterday. "You said that you would always ask for what you wanted."

Luke stroked one of her fingers. "I may not have asked in the way you expected, Olivia, and for that I am sorry—but I have never been shy about asking for what I want. You think your mother just happened to sit you beside me at dinner? You think I actually wanted to make a goddamn wreath? You think your father just decided to take it into his head to invite me here over Christmas?"

Olivia laughed. "I did wonder about that."

"It was you I wanted—want still," said Luke softly, his fingers tightening around hers. "I never thought to ask for you because I have considered you my own for...for so very long."

"And I you," said Olivia shyly. "It feels strange to say these things aloud, after so long, after keeping them to myself."

And yet how right it felt. Sitting here, by the fireside, hand in hand with the man she loved, Olivia could hardly believe it was happening to her. Everything she wanted was coming together; everything she had hoped for in her future, whenever she had made a Christmas wish with the pudding, was here.

Except...

"I told you yesterday," said Olivia shyly, wishing to drop her gaze but forcing herself to hold Luke's own, "that I loved you, but you did not say you loved me. You... asked why I had not said it before."

Luke sighed. "I knew I had made a mistake the moment I said it. I knew what you needed to hear."

Olivia waited, breath caught in her throat, yet nothing seemed forthcoming. "Luke."

"Olivia," Luke said teasingly, and then took a deep breath. "Olivia, I love you. I love you more than I love myself, more than I know what is good for me. I came here to tell you that I loved you, and I was a coward—but no longer, because you make me brave. You make me want to dance with your sister, to make her feel better," and Olivia had to laugh at this, "because I consider her my sister now! Oh, Olivia. You don't even know how much I love you."

CHAPTER TEN

OVERWHELMED, OLIVIA ROSE to her feet—whether to walk away from the gentleman who was giving her so much happiness, happiness she could barely fathom, or toward him to launch herself into his arms, she could barely tell.

It did not seem to matter. Luke did not release her hands, rising himself to pull her into his arms, bestowing upon her the first kiss they shared as two people who had finally, amidst all the confusion and passion they had shared, finally come to an understanding.

Olivia was not sure whether it was merely her mind playing tricks on her, but somehow the kiss felt different. More reverential, yes, but also more passionate. More excited.

More knowledgeable of the things to come.

As Luke's kisses trailed down her neck and his hands moved to her buttocks, Olivia lost herself in the closeness and the understanding they had managed to find together.

"Oh, Olivia. You don't even know how much I love you."

It was precisely what she needed to hear, and in the end, Luke had known that. He had known her better than she had thought, better than she had known herself.

For of course she would have appreciated his help with Katarina in whatever muddle her sister had managed to find herself in. Because he was her family now. Her husband to be.

A husband to be that appeared to be moving very closely to the marital bed, if the strokes and squeezes of his hands on her hips were anything to go by.

"Luke Kingsley," Olivia said laughing, pulling away from Luke just enough to make him concentrate on her words rather than her body. "Is it my imagination, or are you trying to seduce me?"

Luke's pupils were dilated, a lazy smile on his face. "Dear God, if you are only now starting to realize it, I am far worse than I thought."

Olivia chuckled and did not attempt to pull away from his arms. It felt wonderful here, safe, and yet right on the precipice of something not safe at all.

He was dependable, her Luke, and yet dangerous. The best mixture for any man.

"You cannot think what I think you are thinking," she said teasingly.

"I am not sure I follow that at all," said Luke with a chuckle as he kissed her just before her ear, making Olivia's eyelashes flutter, "but if you mean do I want to make love to you here, and now, passionately, making you cry out my name until you explode with pleasure...then yes. Yes, I do."

Olivia's breath caught in her throat at the mere description of what he wanted. It was ridiculous. It was madness! There was no possibility of her giving into such a wild demand.

"Well, dearest one?" Luke said, nuzzling her neck and kissing the tops of her breasts lightly, making it more and more difficult for Olivia to think. "What sort of Christmas gift would you like from me? Do you wish to be touched by me?"

"Yes," breathed Olivia, and then, "Wait—Luke, you cannot mean it! Not now, not here!"

Luke looked up with a shrug. "If we are to be married anyway—wait, you will marry me, won't you?" There was a rather sweet look of brief terror on his face. "I have just realized you did not actually say yes!"

"You did not actually ask me," teased Olivia. "Not the precise words, anyway. I think you said something about 'when we are married'—"

"That is a proposal."

"That is not a proposal!" protested Olivia with a laugh. "And I will certainly not let you do anything more to me if you do not give me the proposal I deserve!"

Not that she was particularly sure she would be able to hold herself back, Olivia thought privately. If Luke kept looking at her like that, and touching her like that, and kissing her there...well, she would not be responsible for her actions.

"Fine!" said Luke, rolling his eyes as he released her with what felt like regret.

Getting down on one knee, he looked up at her with what Olivia could now recognize as adoring eyes. How had she not noticed it before? It felt ridiculous that she should have been in the presence of someone who loved her so much, and she had managed to convince herself that he was doing nothing but teasing her.

"Olivia Fitzroy," Luke said in a deadpan voice. "You are rather beautiful, and ridiculously charming, and I think you like it when I make love to you. Marry me?"

Olivia tapped him on the shoulder. "Not with that attitude!"

"Fine!" Luke grinned. "Dear God, I can't wait for a life with you. And I think that's what...what frightens me the most. The idea of losing you, of not having you. Of you deciding that you deserve better, and you know what, perhaps rightfully so. But I promise to do everything I can to deserve you and earn your trust, and deepen our love. Because I love you, Olivia Fitzroy. Will you please put me out of my misery and agree to be my wife, and let me make love to you."

Olivia flushed. It was going to be a wild life with Luke Kingsley, of that she was sure, if she was not sure of anything else.

But it was a life she wanted. Chalcroft, her family, the Fitzroy gaggle...they were all wonderful, but they could not keep her here when she had the chance to make a new life for herself with Luke.

Here, she was one lady in a line of nine dancing. With him, she was everything. He adored her, she could see that in his eyes. And she rather liked being adored by him.

"I suppose I will," said Olivia with a smile, and then hastily added, "but not here!"

Luke had risen like a jack-in-the-box and kissed her hard on the mouth as soon as she had accepted him. Olivia could feel the hardness of his manhood pressed up against her; he was not joking when he spoke of how much he wanted to make love to her.

And she wanted him. That ache she was starting to know a little too well whenever she was in Luke's presence was starting to build in her, stoked higher and higher as his fingers pulled at her gown, trying to raise her skirts.

"Luke Kingsley!" Olivia said, pulling away from him as she laughed. "You are incorrigible!"

"I am deeply in love with you," said Luke with a grin. "And I want you, Olivia Fitzroy. Badly."

Olivia shivered to hear him say such things.

"Not here," she said, glancing out of the window. There was still a crowd of Fitzroys out there, and some of the outside servants, a few gardeners, appeared to have joined them. Whatever mischief Katarina had managed to get herself into, it appeared she was not able to extricate herself out of it swiftly. "Even with Kitty making a scene...Luke, anyone could come through in here, at any moment!"

"I know," said Luke with a wicked grin. "Exciting, isn't it?"

"Perhaps in the nighttime on a kitchen table," Olivia said firmly. "But not in broad daylight!"

Luke glanced at the window, too, and Olivia could almost see him considering quickly. How much did he want her; how much was he willing to risk?

"You have spoken to my father, haven't you?" asked Olivia

suddenly.

The thought had not crossed her mind until this moment, but now she was Luke's betrothed, it was suddenly very important that he had spoken with her father.

Her papa and she may not see eye to eye on everything, Kitty being one of those topics that they frequently disagreed on, but...

Well. He was her father. He had a right to know that she was being pursued, and was now engaged, to a gentleman he had known for over two decades.

"Fear not," Luke said with a chuckle. "I told you, why do you think I received a sudden invitation to stay at Chalcroft for Christmas?"

Olivia's mouth fell open. "You—you told him that you loved me?"

"Naturally," said Luke brightly. "I have learned never to wait around for love, Olivia. All this dancing about the place, it might have taken you years to realize you loved me."

Olivia punched him lightly on the arm, but Luke took the opportunity to pull her into his embrace. His kisses rained down upon her wildly, causing Olivia to lose all sense of time and place. What did it matter, so long as she was in Luke's arms?

A clatter—a noise outside. A servant had perhaps dropped something, which was unlike them, but it was enough to bring Olivia to her senses.

"Luke Kingsley, you are a bad influence on me," she said ruefully, pulling herself from his arms. "We should—we should go back to the breakfast room, and wait for everyone else to come through. It is the only sensible—"

"Blow that," said Luke. "Come on."

He took her hand, and Olivia followed him without question. With the sensation of his lips crushed on hers so recently, she would have followed him anywhere.

As it was, Luke pulled her into the servants' corridor and then up the stairs. He knew the way. He and Olivia had rushed along here when playing practical jokes on the servants years ago.

Perhaps, Olivia thought wildly, if there was one person in the world who knew Chalcroft just as well as the Fitzroys, it was him.

Luke. An honorary Fitzroy.

"Come on, quietly," he repeated as they reached the main corridor. "This way."

Olivia did not need to ask where they were going. There were only guest bedchambers on this side of the house, and he had been placed in the room he always had whenever he came to visit.

She had always considered it rather mysterious; the dark crimson velvet curtains that lined the windows and the four-poster bed, the softness of the carpet that made it almost impossible to hear when someone was stepping over it.

She was glad of that now. As Luke shut the door behind her and immediately pressed her up against it, Olivia lost herself to the sensations he drew from her.

"I love you," she muttered as Luke broke off his kisses just long enough to pull off his jacket and cravat. "Luke, I love you—"

"I love you, Olivia," he whispered as he pulled off his shirt, revealing a rather handsome torso that made Olivia feel far warmer than she had all day. "Let me love you."

It took but a moment for Luke's scrabbling fingers to find the buttons on the side of Olivia's gown. She was perfectly willing to undo them herself, and perhaps she should have done. Luke's desperate fingers, utterly out of patience, ripped at the fabric, buttons pinging off in all directions.

"Luke!"

"I want you," Luke said in a low voice, lowering his lips to hers but halting just above hers, no matter how high Olivia leaned. "Do you want me?"

"Yes," Olivia breathed, desperation building in her, those lips tantalizingly out of reach. "Yes."

"Tell me you want me."

"I want you," she breathed, unable to think, just to feel, as her gown slipped from her shoulders and pooled to the carpet by her feet. "I want you to touch me, Luke."

He grinned, his fingers moving to the ties of her undershift. "And I want you naked."

"And you."

"Well, you have fingers, don't you?"

Olivia blinked. She did. It had just never occurred to her that now they shared this understanding, now she knew Luke loved her, now they were to be married, to become husband and wife, that she could be a little more bold with him.

That she could share her desires, take charge of them. That she could undress him just as he undressed her.

Fingers shaking a little, Olivia reached out to the buttons on the front of his breeches. They were large, cumbersome, and she found it difficult to concentrate, Luke's fingers brushing down her shoulders as he slowly lowered her undershift.

"I—I can't—"

"Show me," Luke growled as he let her undershift fall to the floor as he placed two hands on either side of her and leaned over her, kissing her neck. "Show me how much you want me."

Olivia ripped the buttons off, pulling the breeches down and releasing Luke's manhood that was already stiff and ready for her.

Luke groaned. "Touch me."

Olivia only hesitated for a moment. He was so beautiful, so ready for her, and it was she who had made him that way. He desired her, and the fact of his desire was so obvious to her now that Olivia wondered how she could ever have mistaken it before.

Trembling slightly, she reached out and touched Luke's manhood slowly. It was warm, wet at the tip, and without being told, Olivia knew what to do. Grasping it with increasing tightness, she moved her hand so that the wetness spread down him, making it slicker, easier to stroke.

Luke shuddered as he leaned against the door. "Olivia, I love it when you—oh, yes, yes…"

She kissed him then, kissed him full on the mouth, captured his lips with her own as he had captured her heart. They would always be together, always. Olivia knew that no matter what happened, they would be together.

"Stop!"

Startled, Olivia dropped his manhood which stayed upright. "Did I hurt—did I do something wrong?"

There was a glaze of desire across Luke's eyes as he smiled. "No, Olivia, you were perfect—too perfect."

Olivia swallowed. "Then I want you inside me. Now."

He did not need much invitation. Picking her up by her buttocks and leaning her against the door, her legs wrapped around him, Luke slowly entered her.

"Luke!"

"Olivia!"

It was like coming home. Olivia would have wept if she was not so warm with desire, so desperate for Luke to take her once again on that sweet journey that led to such ecstasy.

"Love me," she begged, clutching his shoulders. "Love me."

Luke's strength made it possible. As he lifted her, thrusting into her and bringing Olivia closer and closer to the edge of the ecstasy which she thirsted for so desperately, she clung to him, clung to the one man she knew she would adore for the rest of her life.

"Yes, yes, more," Olivia panted, ignoring the thumping of their lovemaking against the door, sure no one would hear them. "Luke!"

"Olivia!"

He crashed into her, pouring himself into her, surely causing bruises to her back, but Olivia did not care. She threw herself to the wind, casting all abandon aside as she clutched the man she loved, as the carnal pleasures they enjoyed ripped through her, making her body shake with pleasure.

Luke balanced her between his body and the door, and Olivia slowly, when she felt as though the room had stopped spinning and the world had come back into focus, lowered her legs to the floor.

"That…that was…"

"I know," she whispered. Olivia brushed back that curl of hair from Luke's forehead, and laughed. "If you're not too careful, Lord Luke Kingsley, you will exhaust me doing that."

Luke chuckled dryly. "Well, future Lady Olivia Kingsley, I might just do that. I want to know when I dance with you this evening, that I have first quite thoroughly worn you out." He kissed her on the cheek.

Olivia captured his mouth with hers and gave herself to the kiss, allowing his tongue to tease her own, arching her back against him and loving the sensation of her breasts against his chest.

"Dancing?" she whispered with a laugh. "You think I'll be able to stand long enough for a single dance?"

Luke smiled, and Olivia's heart sang with happiness. "We'll dance every day of the rest of our lives."

About Emily E K Murdoch

If you love falling in love, then you've come to the right place.

I am a historian and writer and have a varied career to date: from examining medieval manuscripts to designing museum exhibitions, to working as a researcher for the BBC to working for the National Trust.

My books range from England 1050 to Texas 1848, and I can't wait for you to fall in love with my heroes and heroines!

Follow me on twitter and instagram @emilyekmurdoch, find me on facebook at facebook.com/theemilyekmurdoch, and read my blog at www.emilyekmurdoch.com.